# Savage's Trap

When Savage was assigned to uncover evidence against Max Chaney and bring him to trial, he had no idea of the danger he was riding into. Chaney, a Californian politician, was suspected of killing a US marshal, and he had Gruber's gang on hand to wipe out any opposition in the run-up to his election as state governor.

Surviving an attempt on his life, Savage isleft in a coma. Cared for by Dr Perry and a nurse called Tulip, he recovers to find himself hunted by Gruber's gang and the police.

Savage's only chance is to bide his time until he can set and spring the trap that will end Chaney's reign of terror.

# Savage's Trap

SYDNEY J. BOUNDS

**A Black Horse Western**

ROBERT HALE · LONDON

© Sydney J. Bounds 2005
First published in Great Britain 2005

ISBN 0 7090 7730 0

Robert Hale Limited
Clerkenwell House
Clerkenwell Green
London EC1R 0HT

Typeset by
Derek Doyle & Associates, Shaw Heath.
Printed and bound in Great Britain by
Antony Rowe Limited, Wiltshire

# CONTENTS

# CHAPTER 1

## Unmarked Graves

'Not boring you, am I?'

The words stabbed like an ice pick and Allan Pinkerton jerked upright in the too-comfortable armchair and forced his eyes open.

'No, Senator, I'm just tired from the journey. It's been a long day, and I'm not as young as I was.'

Senator Wilmot's face creased in a smile, and he quoted the motto of the private detective agency: 'We never sleep.'

'True, but note the "We". I sleep, while others work for me.'

Pinkerton felt he could sleep right now. The air was close and the meal had run to four courses. He stifled a yawn.

The room was small, above one of the quieter restaurants in Washington. The walls were panelled and varnished, the furnishings elegant and a fire burned in the grate. Beyond the windows, draped with heavy curtains, a cold wind whistled. A lamp glowed on a small table placed between the two men. It was a room borrowed for a special occasion.

Pinkerton smoothed out his beard and tried to project an air of alertness. 'You were telling me about Chaney.'

Wilmot looked as though politicking in the capital had sucked his body dry, leaving him a shrivelled up shell, faded and prejudiced. He was, Pinkerton knew, an honest man – at least as honest as a politician could be – and he owed the senator a favour. He concentrated on listening.

'Max Chaney,' Wilmot said, 'is dangerous. A power-mad crazy man who aims to be the next gover-nor of California and isn't fussy about the methods he uses. He has already hinted that his next step will bring him to the Senate. And it would not surprise me if he had an eye on the White House.'

'So?'

'A group of us arranged for a US marshal named Jarvis to watch him, and we've had regular reports. Now we hear nothing and Jarvis is missing. We fear he is dead.'

'You're suggesting that Chaney killed a US marshal?'

'Not personally. He has a bodyguard, a redheaded gunman named Boyd. And there is a bunch of roughs who, apparently, take their orders directly from Chaney – their main job appears to be scaring off any opposition.'

Pinkerton frowned. 'Interesting, even worrying, but surely one bullet is all that's necessary? I can—'

'No! I agree, he could be stopped that way, but I want to use him as an example. There are others of his stamp who, if allowed to gain positions of authority, would put an end to any notion of democracy in this country.'

Wilmot paused to pour water from a carafe into a glass and eased his throat.

'I need an undercover agent to seek out evidence that will bring him to trial and convict Chaney in a court of law.'

'You have access to other marshals, and I think they would—'

'Jarvis was betrayed, I suspect – perhaps by a leak in Washington.'

'There are plenty of wagging tongues here,' Pinkerton agreed.

'So I hope you will be able to send one of your men to Sacramento, Allan. Nobody will know except you and me. That's why I've kept our meeting secret.'

Pinkerton hesitated. 'It's not a good idea to let anyone get away with murdering a lawman, I agree with you there, Senator, but—'

'We have to insist on respect for the law, Allan, and this would be quite unofficial.'

Pinkerton smiled faintly. 'Naturally. And I think I know the man for this . . . he seems to have a blind eye for anything official.'

*

With an echoing clanging of iron against iron, a squeal of brakes and hiss of steam, the huge locomotive gradually eased to a stop. Behind it, carriage doors were flung open and carpet bags and bedrolls thrown out.

Men tumbled on to the wooden platform like prisoners released from jail; even the steam horse took time to cross the continent from east to west. Porters shifted heavy trunks and, for a few minutes, there was a confusion of greetings, questions and answers, and curses.

During the chaos of noise and smoky dust, Savage made a quiet exit, carrying his shotgun and saddlebag. He was small and agile and was hardly noticed as he eased through the crowd.

He passed a station sign bearing the name FOLSOM, and another advertising a circus COMING SOON and reached the end of the platform where it joined a muddy street sloping down to a river.

He saw a string of mules loaded with ore, stores that were simply enlarged cabins, a livery stable, saloons and dining-rooms. He paused briefly, tugging down his hat as an icy wind tried to lift it. No one seemed interested in him so he headed for a hardware store claiming to have miners' supplies.

A smiling storeman watched him enter and approach the counter.

'Trying your luck, sir? We've got all you need to

succeed – tin pan, pick and shovel, overalls, boots. . . .'

'Boots?'

'Surely.' The storeman brought a pair from below the counter. 'Wooden soles and leather uppers – panning is a wet job, sir, standing in water all day, or slipping on mud.'

'You'll know,' Savage agreed.

'Right,' the storeman said blandly. 'We've outfitted hundreds of prospectors. More miners have been successful with our equipment than that of any other store.'

Savage brought a gold piece from his pocket and paid.* The storeman added, 'The stable across the way can provide a mule.'

Savage carried his gear to the livery and black-smith's barn, where a brawny man glanced at him and yawned. 'A mule, is it?'

Savage knew something about mules and took his time making his choice. Satisfied, he led the animal to another store and stocked up with bacon, beans and salt, coffee and sugar. He was now almost an old hand at camping in the wild.

On the way out of Folsom he stopped at an eating-house; it might be a while before he got a decent meal again.

He didn't hurry with his chops and potatoes and pie and lingered over a mug of coffee, waiting for the

* See *Savage – Manhunter*, Robert Hale, 2004.

evening shadows to arrive. When he finally left town, he was reasonably sure no one was watching him; he was only another latecomer aiming to try his hand at panning for gold.

He followed the river till the lights of town disappeared, climbed a rise to find dry ground and bedded down for the night among a cluster of oaks, out of the wind.

The morning air was clear and carried the chill of winter. Savage washed but left his stubble to grow. He made breakfast and then urged his mule along the river-bank to a suitably isolated spot for a first attempt at panning.

The water was icy, tumbling down from the distant Sierra mountains and soon his back was aching and his hands numb. This was hard work and he figured he wasn't going to get rich in a hurry.

'Reckon you're new to this game,' a voice croaked, and he looked up at his audience, a man of about fifty with a rust-brown beard, a battered hat and a long mud-streaked coat.

'True,' Savage said, 'and I guess they call you Rusty.'

'You've got that right. For a drink, I'll give yuh a few tips.'

'I don't carry a bottle. Suppose we make it the price of a drink?'

Rusty's weathered face brightened. 'That'll do me. Give me that pan.'

12

The old man waded into the stream. 'It's no good trying to keep dry on this job. Get in the water and scoop up the bottom, like this.' He demonstrated. 'Now rotate the pan so the water swirls around and flows over the lip of the pan . . . see the water carries away the lighter dirt and leaves the heavy stuff behind. Gold is heavy.'

Rusty climbed up on to the river bank and gave the pan back to Savage. 'This area has been over-worked, so you won't find much anyway. Move along a bit and try it.'

Savage stepped into freezing water and imitated his action, while Rusty commented.

'Keep your pan flat, or you'll chuck the yellow stuff out with the dirt . . . that's better. Don't hurry, and try to work up a rhythm.'

While Savage panned, the old man began to relive his past. 'I remember when there were diggings all along this river. And tents pegged down beside the shallows, wagons bringing up liquor and food, served from plank counters in the open . . . all gone now.'

Savage straightened and shoved numbed hands into his his pockets to revive them.

Rusty rambled on: 'You'll need to find a place that hasn't been overworked and stake a claim. Watch out for the Chinese – they came along after us, to pick over our leavings. But earlier, I've seen nuggets as big as your fist taken out of pans – now, us prospectors have mostly gone since the big operators moved in.'

Savage started to scramble out, slipped and got

mud on his clothes. He swore. 'Seems like I'm wasting my time here . . . say, did you ever hear of a fella called Jarvis?'

Rusty lifted his hat, revealing a freckled skull, and scratched. 'Jarvis? No, I can't say I've heard that name.'

'He might not have got this far. Last I heard he'd reached Sacramento.'

'Waal, now, there's folk who run foul of the boss man there and don't get heard from again. Let me show yuh something.'

Savage loaded his gear on to the mule and followed the oldster further along the river-bank. Rusty paused when he reached a row of low mounds that were no more than bumps in the mud.

'Graves,' he said. 'D'yuh see any names? Where there's gold there's killing, and a bunch of unmarked graves. Who knows who's in 'em? Maybe your friend Jarvis is in one!'

'That could be,' Savage agreed.

Rusty shifted from one foot to another. 'All this talking sure gives a man a thirst.'

Savage handed him a dollar and the old prospector scooted for the nearest saloon.

Savage smiled, satisfied. It was easy now to understand how a US marshal could go missing. He urged his mule on at a steady pace, following the bed of the river, until he saw a group of Chinese panning the shallows.

He stopped to watch them and saw no wasted

14

motion; they worked smoothly and fast and seemed to be getting some yellow dust. He noted buckskin bags stacked under low brush with a man on guard.

He pushed the mule down the slope. The guard came upright, long-bladed knife in hand, calling in his own language to the other miners.

Savage stopped and held both hands out to show they were empty. 'Sure admire the way you people work. I'm just wondering if, maybe, I could buy a bag of that dust from you?'

They closed about him, excited. Savage remained calm. Only once before had he met Chinese, and then Wing Fat had been helpful.

'Buy?' The one with the blade remained suspicious. Obviously this group had been given a bad time by some Americans.

Carefully he brought out a minted gold piece from his pocket and offered it. A Chinaman inspected it, bit it between his teeth and then held up three fingers. Savage gave him another two coins to test.

They were all smiling now. A Yankee fool, obviously. One picked up a bag of dust and handed it to him with a flourish.

Savage opened it, fingered the small yellow grains, tightened the drawstring and put the bag in his pocket.

The knife man lowered his blade. 'Good?'

Savage nodded. 'A deal.'

He climbed on his mule and headed west.

Eventually he came to Sacramento, unshaven, his clothes streaked with mud; just another prospector who'd given up the gold trail.

# CHAPTER 2

# THE MAN FROM TEXAS

Sacramento was a town pretending to be a city and Savage, originally from New York, was not impressed. It was bigger than many western towns he'd ridden through and boasted brick and stone buildings, some with two storeys. But the lower end of town was the usual jumble of frame houses, hovels and discarded garbage; some backstreets did not even have boardwalks. A familiar smell composed of rotting vegetables and dead rats hung over the poorer areas.

As his mule plodded past a pawnshop, a gaudy poster caught his eye and he halted long enough to read it.

EVERETT'S CIRCUS
Now you can see a real elephant!
Lion acts and daredevils on the high wire!
Clowns and stunts on the trapeze!
Thrills and laughs for young and old!
Bareback riding, etc, etc.
For two weeks only – book early.
**BOOK NOW!**

Behind him, a voice drawled, 'Guess you ain't seen anything like that before, huh? But this here's the west coast, the capital of California, and we've got everything, and more.'

Savage turned his head slowly, just looking and not saying anything. His memory was still conjuring up images of sneaking under a canvas big top in New York to see a circus when he was a kid.

The speaker was dressed as a cowboy with Stetson, high heeled boots and a Colt revolver slung low. While most men were miners, dockers or townsmen in suits, he stood out like a finger in splints.

'I'd like to see the show,' Savage admitted.

'Then you won't want to waste money on some fancy hotel. I can recommend Ma Hubbard's, where I'm staying.'

'Why not? I'm not the richest ex-miner to hit town.'

'That figures. My name's Doyle. Jim Doyle, from Texas, and I ain't exactly flush either. Just waiting for a herd from the south-west to arrive and hoping to get a job with one of the buyers.'

Savage nodded politely. Doyle appeared to be a bit of a dandy with his silk neckerchief and handmade boots that fitted like another skin. His hands were not those of a man who'd worked cattle.

'This way,' the Texan said, and led off.

Savage followed, past saloons and stores and gambling halls, restaurants and cafés. There was a church and a school-house.

'Ma's a good cook so I advise taking full board. Her partner takes care of the laundry, so . . .' Doyle shrugged.

'All the home comforts?' Savage suggested.

Doyle nodded, and pointed into an alley. 'That way to the port, if you're thinking of the river.'

'Why should I think of the river? I just got here.'

'Waal, this town doesn't suit everyone. Some find it kind of unhealthy and leave in a hurry.'

Savage noticed a livery stable and turned and rode inside. Doyle waited.

'I'm quitting the diggings,' Savage told the stable-man. 'What'll you give me for the mule?' He dismounted and removed the saddle and the stable-man walked around the animal, inspecting its points critically and prodding with a horny finger.

'Guess I can let you have something. It won't be much though.'

'I'll take any offer.'

The man gave him a couple of dollars. When Doyle drawled from the doorway, 'Robbery', he added one more.

Savage pocketed the money, picked up his saddle-bag and shotgun and walked outside.

Doyle gestured at the gun. 'D'yuh use that thing?'

'When necessary.'

They walked on, past a stagecoach office and a hardware store till Doyle said, 'Here we are.'

A sign read: HUBBARD'S CUPBOARD.

This was a wooden house of two storeys, the bottom half old and leaning, the upper half newly added on. It looked top-heavy.

As the cowboy opened the door, Savage murmured, 'I hope the cupboard's not bare.'

'No fear of that,' a brisk voice answered, and Savage saw a solidly built woman with a broom in her hands. 'Mr Doyle, tell your friend about the meals here.'

'Enough on each plate for two starving cowpokes and the finest quality,' he replied promptly.

Savage touched the brim of his hat and offered the bag of gold dust. 'Name's Savage, ma'am.'

Ma Hubbard weighed the bag in her hand. 'It'll do for now, but you'd best start looking for paid work. I don't feed vagrants.' She looked him over and sniffed. 'The wash-house is out back.'

'Yes, ma'am,' Savage said meekly.

'House rules – no drunkenness and no loose women on the premises.' Belatedly, she added, 'Welcome to Hubbard's Cupboard.' She raised her voice. 'Here, J.C. We've got a new boarder.'

A small thin Chinese man appeared in the passage

behind her, bowing and smiling. 'Welcome, sir.'

The woman said, 'Me and J.C. are partners, so you mind what he tells you.'

'This way, sir.'

Savage followed the Chinaman up wooden stairs to a small room with a bed and a chair. He dropped his gear. A meal, he decided, and sleep. Tomorrow would be soon enough to start investigating Max Chaney.

After breakfast, Savage asked the way to the news-paper office and set off unhurriedly for the *Sacramento Union*. Carefully shaven and wearing a coat to cover his Bowie, he looked a different man from the loser who'd hit town yesterday.

He'd left his shotgun in his room and Doyle, he noted, was not present at the breakfast-table.

To the young lady fronting the office, he said, 'I'd like a word with the editor.'

She opened her mouth wide and yelled, 'Dad, customer!' She smiled at him, young and attractive, with her fair hair in curls.

A muttering that might have been cuss words came from a backroom. The metallic clanking of a hand-press stopped and a man stepped through the door-way, wiping his hands on a piece of rag. He wore glasses and chewed on the stem of a pipe that had gone out.

'Fred Hooper. Where are you from? D'you have a story for me?'

'Savage, from the East, and no story. I'm looking for information.'

Hooper snatched up a copy of the *Union* from a table and thrust it at him. 'Read all about it, with my compliments. You'll have to excuse me—'

'I may have some money to invest—'

'Insert an ad with my daughter for quick results.'

'Someone mentioned a name. Chaney. Can you tell me anything about him?'

Hooper's attitude changed, his face clouded with suspicion. 'Who put you up to this? Or are you new in town?'

'I arrived yesterday.'

Hooper gave him a searching look, and came to an abrupt decision. 'Come into the back room. Alice, see we're not disturbed.'

The small room was crowded, a hand press and stacks of paper taking up most of it. There was a smell of ink and oil.

Hooper said, 'Chaney is an important man in this city – he'd like you to think, *the* important man. I walk a knife edge where his affairs are concerned – I'm expected to report them but not criticize. I intend to stay in business, Mr Savage, so I need to be careful what I say in print. If you repeat anything I tell you, I shall deny it.'

Hooper reamed out the bowl of his pipe and began to ram tobacco into it.

'I've already been warned by his bully-boys but, like any tyrant, he won't last for ever. If I outlast him, and I intend to, I can print what everyone knows, and more. So, if you have genuine business with him, be careful what you say in public. And don't go around asking questions – that's one thing he won't stand for.'

Savage managed to look sceptical. 'So what's he done that's so bad?'

Hooper struck a match for his pipe and got it going.

'He levies a tax – a quite unofficial tax – on local businesses, and a bunch of toughs collects it for him. The police turn a blind eye. He owns shares in the Central Pacific Railroad, which means his reach spreads out from here. And has shares in some of the bigger gold mines; these bring in money to pay his gang. He scares a lot of people in this city, and now he's running for governor.'

The room seemed to be filling with smoke. The editor murmured, 'Step warily, Mr Savage, or you might just disappear, as others have.'

Savage raised an eyebrow. 'Thanks for the tip.'

On the way out, he nodded to the girl and continued along the street. It occurred to him it was not going to be easy to get anyone to testify against Max Chaney.

He moved on till he came to a red-and-white striped pole projecting above a shop front. If there was one thing a barber was noted for it was bending ears. Savage walked inside and dropped into a chair in front of a mirror.

'Feels like I'm getting shaggy around the back of the neck. Give it a trim so I'm fit for civilized society again.'

'Of course, sir. From the East, are we?'

'New York.'

Deftly the barber tossed Savage's hat on to a peg and began snipping with a pair of scissors. 'Just visiting, are we, sir?'

'On business,' Savage said, watching the barber in the mirror. 'I might be doing business with somone called Chaney. Can you tell me anything about him?'

The barber lifted the scissors away from Savage's neck as if they had become red-hot, and darted a look towards the doorway.

'If you can take a hint, sir, it's best not to indulge in loose talk about Max Chaney. He carries weight, and tends to resent anyone asking personal questions.'

He finished in a hurry and Savage paid, put on his hat and left. It seemed Chaney's toughs had the locals thoroughly intimidated.

He passed a bank and a wooden house being torn down; workmen were bringing up a cartload of bricks to start rebuilding something more permanent. Just beyond, a uniformed policeman stood on the corner of the street, looking into an alley. Passersby crossed to the opposite side of the road.

Savage paused beside the policeman who advised, 'Move along, before they see you.'

Savage ignored the advice. He watched three men with clubs studded with nails beating on a man who had been disarmed. One of the gang, squat with long arms and resembling an ape stood apart, eyes gleaming as he encouraged the beating.

'Give it to him, Smelly – these pikers have got to learn to pay up.'

The man doing the beating grunted and laid into the victim with fresh energy. Blood streaked the battered and bruised face. Two of the gang propped up Smelly's target, who appeared to have lost the use of one arm trying to fend off earlier blows.

'Shouldn't you be stopping this?' Savage asked the lawman.

The officer glanced at him. 'You must be a visitor. Those men take their orders from Mr Chaney, and the law doesn't apply to him.'

The beaten man began to sob. 'No more, no more. I'll pay!'

'See that you do, and before sunset.'

The apeman turned away and saw Savage watching.

'What d'you want? Stick your nose in our business and you'll get it sliced off.'

'I'm told you work for Mr Chaney,' Savage said calmly. 'I may have some business for him, so maybe you can point me to his office?'

The apeman moved swiftly towards Savage and the policeman stepped back, leaving him alone.

'You're the one asking questions, ain't yuh? The boss wants to talk to you.'

Smelly hurried up and Savage learnt how he'd got his name; likely he hadn't washed for a month. Smelly brandished his club, the nails wet with blood and torn skin.

'This one next, Gruber?' he asked eagerly.

'Not yet. The boss wants him.'

Members of the gang surrounded Savage, leaving their victim huddled on the ground.

Gruber said, 'Go,' and Savage found himself hustled towards the river.

The alley led, via a dogleg, to the port, busy with shipping; jetties were piled high with goods being loaded on to carts and mules by men who avoided looking directly at the gang.

Savage smelled rotting fish and spilled spices and sewage.

Gruber ignored the dock workers and headed directly towards a building set apart from the rest; it was built on piers and projected out over the water. A faded sign read: *Oil, Paint, Cordage, Canvas.*

At one time, Savage guessed, this had been a chandler's store and saw that an upper storey had been added.

Gruber pushed open the door and urged Savage inside. More roughs sat around, drinking, smoking and watching a card game. He noted a trapdoor set in the floor planks and reflected how easy it would be to lose a body in the river.

A flight of stairs led to the second storey. Gruber gestured at him: 'Up, go up.'

Savage smiled faintly; it seemed the fly was invited into the spider's web.

# CHAPTER 3

## A MATTER OF TRUST

The door at the top of the stairs was closed and Savage heard the sound of a voice beyond, but not clearly enough to make out the words.

Behind him, Gruber said, 'Knock once and wait.' Savage ignored him. He pushed open the door and walked in.

Gruber cursed. 'I told him, boss!'

The man seated in a swivel chair behind the desk went on talking as if there had been no interruption. At his back stood a tall thin man with a head of red hair; he had watchful eyes, a nose like a blade and a revolver appeared in his hand in one swift movement.

Savage recognized the type: a gun for hire, and guessed this was Boyd.

The room was sparsely furnished: a bed, a wooden

27

table with washbowl and mirror, a wardrobe and wood-burning stove. Chaney, it seemed, rejected the trappings of wealth. There was a single window but otherwise only the one way in or out.

The man standing before the desk looked a solid citizen in a business suit and yet he was completely cowed; he had been reduced to a small boy waiting for a beating.

'You now owe the house five thousand dollars.' Chaney's voice was flat yet held subtle menace.

'And you know what will happen if you fail to pay.' His grimace could have been a smile, the smile of a cat about to pounce. 'But this is your lucky day – you will persuade every one of your employees to vote for me in the coming election and I will extend your credit by another thousand. You may continue to play your favourite game of chance. For now.'

'Thank you, Mr Chaney, I'll speak to my people right away.' The debtor ducked his head and hurried from the room, his shoes echoing on the stairs.

Gruber waited a moment for Chaney to focus his gaze on Savage, then said, 'This is the fella you wanted, boss. The one asking questions.'

Max Chaney took his time looking him over. 'Asking questions. Behind my back. If you want to know anything about me, ask me – now I want to know about you.'

'Name's Savage. I came West in a bit of a hurry when the New York police started to take a little too much interest.'

'On the run then.' Chaney continued to stare into his face with eyes as black as his hair, showing no emotion.

'I thought we might deal—'

'No, Mr Savage, no deals. Convince me you have something, anything, I need, then I'll buy and you deliver. Is someone paying you to ask questions?'

Savage made a small smile. 'Not yet.'

'I'm going to need all the votes I can get, and I'm paying a dollar a vote.'

Chaney rose from his chair and lurched towards him; there was something wrong with his legs that prevented him walking normally.

He peeled a five-dollar bill from a roll of notes and held it out. 'You'll be given four other names to use on the day.'

Savage realized he was no taller than himself, but there was an intensity about him that would frighten some men. He took the note and tucked it in his shirt pocket.

Chaney gave him a lingering stare, chilled as a fish on a slab of ice. 'You've taken my money and that makes you my man. You're bought and paid for – forget that and it'll be your life. Where are you stay-ing? Just so I can find you.'

'Ma Hubbard's.'

Chaney retreated to his seat. 'You get a discount at any of my saloons, parlours, eating places – now stop asking questions.'

Savage went downstairs and out on the dockside

and thought about Chaney, a man with big ideas; but so had others been and where were they now? It seemed that, for the moment, he was on the inside and free to act.

He stood watching the gulls and the boats come upriver, unload and depart. A young woman passed by and attracted his attention, reminding him he was watered and fed and had money in his pocket. Maybe he'd find himself a woman and the thought came; take a look at one of Chaney's parlours. Likely his would be the best in town if he was using them to hook the self-important.

He started walking, and had only to use his eyes. It was a large house of new brick, the windows covered by red and purple drapes, discreetly set back from the sidewalk behind a screen of bushes.

He used an ornately carved knocker and the door was promptly opened by a small Negro boy dressed in a splendid uniform. 'Yes, sir?'

'Mr Chaney sent me.'

The boy gave a toothy smile and stepped back. 'Welcome to Madame Irene's, sir.'

Inside, the air was perfumed and a wall-to-wall bar filled the rear of a large room. Young women, in their underwear, sat around waiting for clients. Gold-framed mirrors reflected them in the light thrown by candles set in silver holders.

The boy brought him a glass of wine, but Savage waved it away. 'Not for me. I'm not here to drink.' And he might need all his faculties later.

A stout woman, smartly dressed and with her hair up, approached with the air of a businesswoman. 'I am Madame Irene and this is my establishment. Do you have a recommendation?'

'Mr Chaney—'

She cut him short with an abrupt gesture of a hand heavily ornamented by rings. 'Perhaps. Anyone can walk in and use a well-known name. This establishment is run on a cash-only basis, payment in advance.'

Savage gave her a gold eagle. Her eyes opened wide as she tested it. 'Waal, now, you just take your pick of my beauties.'

He had already made his choice; the youngest, a small Chinese in an outsize shift sitting on a sofa.

'Mary,' she said, rising from her seat. 'Follow behind on stairs please.' She raised her shift to show a pert bottom.

There was a corridor at the top with doors opening on to small rooms. Mary's room held a single bed stripped down to a mattress, a washbowl on a stand and a towel; no red plush here.

She pulled her shift up over her head, folded it and placed in under the pillow. She perched on the edge of the bed, legs slightly parted; she had small breasts and a sly smile.

'American curious about Asian gal, yes?'

Savage didn't answer. He dropped his pants and stepped out of them. It had been a while since his last woman and he was ready.

Mary lay back and he climbed aboard her. Her fingers skilfully guided him, encouraging him to pump away until he collapsed in exhaustion.

He lay back, relieved and satisfied, and she reached under the bed for a cigarette and struck a match.

'You are pleased with Mary, yes?'

'Sure.' Savage washed quickly and dressed and handed her a gold piece. 'For you. Hide it away some place – I've a few questions for you.'

'Questions?' She giggled. 'What you think Mary know that white American don't?' She lit another cigarette from the butt of the first, watching him, her head cocked to one side and bright-eyed.

'I think you hear a lot of pillow talk. Maybe about this man Chaney who seems to run the town. You know him?'

'Big time man, sure. Own this house, also much property. Likes to give orders all the time.'

'So what's he like as a man?'

She pulled a face. 'No like. Cold, uncaring person. He no want women. Only want to control people.' She shivered. 'No respect for money . . . only power!'

When Savage left Madame Irene's, grey clouds scudded overhead, and darkness came early as autumn merged into an early winter. The wind cut chill and he walked briskly, heading towards Hubbard's Cupboard for the evening meal. Mary seemed to have unlocked his appetite for food.

The residents of the boarding-house were seated

around the table in the dining-room, waiting. It seemed almost like a family gathering, he thought.

Doyle, the cowboy, was doing most of the talking, and the light from an oil lamp showed that his face was flushed. 'Lady luck ran with me,' he crowed, 'and I won a bundle at the poker table.'

So that's how he manages, Savage thought. The other boarders nodded to him; they looked weary. Probably dock workers, he decided.

Ma Hubbard and her Chinese partner served up large platters filled with mutton pie and potatoes, then sat down with their boarders. There were already thick chunks of bread and two large jugs of water on the table.

Ma said, 'For what we are about to eat, we thank our good Lord.'

There was silence till every plate was cleared and gravy mopped up; eating was serious business. They waited for J.C. to bring in the pudding.

Savage said, 'I noticed there's an election coming up. Who's standing against this fella Chaney?'

Ma Hubbard spoke briskly. 'No politics at the meal table. That's a thing I won't put up with.'

'Yes, ma'am,' Savage said meekly.

When he finished his raisin pudding and coffee, he felt sleepy and went up to his room. Doyle followed him up and Savage went into his room, leaving the door open. He wondered what was coming.

The Texan leaned against the door frame, looking in. 'You really interested in this election?'

Savage shrugged. 'Just curious. It looks like Chaney has no opposition, and I find that odd.'

'Waal, you're new here. Chaney more or less runs this town, so . . . Fowler is the name you're looking for, but you won't find him here. He started as store-keeper and grew; he's big time now, with more than one store, but he lives in San Francisco and stays there.'

'Safer,' Savage murmured.

'Maybe so. Some say Chaney plays rough.'

'I heard.'

Doyle loosened his silk neckerchief. 'If you're interested, Fowler keeps an office here. His support-ers handle posters and handbills and stuff.'

'I might look in.'

Doyle straightened up and nodded. 'I made more than my daily dollar today, so I'll have an early night.'

He walked along the passage to his own room and closed the door after him.

Upstairs in Chaney's office-home above the old chan-dler's store, Gruber said, 'Savage is still asking ques-tions. Let me work on him, boss – I've a guaranteed cure for a loose tongue. Rip it out!'

Boyd, standing behind Chaney, kept quiet and listened to the lapping of the river against the piers. It was a peaceful sound; any time the rhythm changed he came alert.

The front of the wood-burning stove was open, throwing out a cherry-red glow. The man in the chair at the desk sat unmoving, his face without expression. If he felt any emotion it didn't show by speech or movement. He could have been dozing.

Eventually, Chaney looked at the apelike man and said flatly, 'No.'

He paused and when he continued it was as if he was speaking to himself. 'He took my money. When I buy a man I trust him to stay bought. He has broken that trust.'

He swivelled his chair to stare at his bodyguard, and now fury bubbled beneath his cold exterior. The rage leaking from his eyes made even Boyd uneasy.

'Kill him, Boyd. Kill Savage! His death must serve as an example to any who cannot be trusted. Take time to set it up carefully – make it a public execution!'

# CHAPTER 4

## HEADSHOT

Fowler's local supporters had taken over an empty shop in an area scheduled for rebuilding. On his way there, Savage saw VOTE FOWLER posters had been torn down and stickers defaced. It appeared that Max Chaney's hired men actively discouraged any show by his opposition.

The morning air was on the chill side and he walked with a swing. He estimated he was halfway to Fowler's office when he heard the explosion, and paused; the few people about ignored it. Blasting powder, he decided, and continued on his way. Ahead he saw a rising cloud of dust and smoke and the red glow of flames.

A bell *clanged* vigorously and a voice bawled, 'Fire!' There were still many wooden buildings in the city and so the situation had to be taken seriously.

A fire pump rushed past him, bright red with polished brass and gold lettering: Fire Engine Co. No. 1. It was pulled by four men and they were running.

'Make way, make way!'

Savage slowed his pace when he recognized one of Gruber's gang, a broad smile on his face, moving away from the flames. He took his time, guessing he was already too late to visit Fowler's headquarters.

Hoses snaked from the river, but the men manning the pump were content to soak nearby buildings to stop the fire spreading.

He spoke to the fire chief, who stood with his hands behind his back, staring at the shell of a shop and still smouldering paper. 'Arson?'

The fire chief turned to scrutinize him. 'For the record, stranger, purely accidental. This will come under the heading of land clearance.'

'Any casualties?'

'We shan't know that until the debris cools enough to start a search.'

'But you will make a search?'

'A search won't do a lot for anyone caught in that, will it?'

'I wonder who might be interested in developing this bit of land?'

'If you're interested in land, speak to Mr Chaney.'

'Maybe I will.'

Savage turned away and walked back towards the town centre; a few shoppers paused to stare at the pall of smoke, but no one investigated or asked questions aloud. He considered his options: visit the chief of police – or did Chaney already have him on his payroll? Perhaps a visit to a banker might produce a more interesting result?

From the *Sacramento Union*:

> This paper believes it is the duty of every Californian to vote in the coming gubernatorial election and to vote according to his convictions. This paper wishes to emphasize that your vote is secret with no one looking over your shoulder. Ignore the ballyhoo and vote for whoever you want.
>
> Now is the time to register a protest against the present upsurge in violence, to choose a governor who will represent your interests and who will run this state the way you want. You know the candidates and we urge you, one and all, to make your choice according to your conscience. Make your decision felt in the voting booth!'

Max Chaney slammed down the latest edition of the *Union* on the counter where Alice Hooper sat.

'Tell your father if there is any more of this fence-sitting, there will be trouble.'

Alice forced a smile. 'I'll tell—'

'You can leave my daughter out of this.' The editor

and owner of the newspaper stepped quietly from the back room. 'Tell me yourself if you have a complaint.'

Chaney said flatly, 'I don't complain. I give orders. You will print what I tell you or regret it.'

Behind him, Boyd shifted uneasily. Why couldn't Alice's father be sensible?

Chaney's cold stare shifted from the editor to his daughter. 'How would it be if I found a place for her in Madame Irene's. Do you think she would earn her keep? Or would she need special training?'

Fred Hooper's face turned grey. His hands knotted. 'You lay a finger on Alice, Chaney, and I'll kill you!'

Chaney glanced at his red-haired bodyguard. 'D'you think you'll have any difficulty with this one?'

Boyd's hatchet face creased in a frown. 'No difficulty, Mr Chaney.'

Hooper looked sick.

Chaney continued in an icy tone, 'Who would look after your daughter if you met with an accident? Think seriously about this, Hooper, then support me in your paper.'

Max Chaney left with a warm glow. He liked to see the righteous crawl, and had learned long ago to use fear like a cattle prod.

Boyd touched his hat to Alice and followed his boss outside.

*

Savage had read the *Union*'s editorial too, and wondered if it was worth trying Hooper again.

He was crossing a square where some enthusiast had started to make a public garden; after rain, it was just a patch of churned-up mud.

The tables outside a restaurant were deserted; the cold and damp had driven customers inside. He was close by a theatre, overlooked by the clock tower, when a voice called: 'You there . . . I want to talk to you.'

Savage saw a cripple supported on two sticks crossing the square towards him, and paused.

The cripple said, 'Talk to me and I'll tell you what yuh want to know. Anything. Everything. I heard you were asking about Chaney and I can tell yuh plenty. I'm not afraid of him. How I was beat up and left for dead. What he's done to people I know, just ask me and—'

Savage started to walk towards him and, when he stopped, was close enough to smell whiskey on the man's breath.

'I was one who spoke out against Max Chaney.' The cripple sounded bitter. 'I'm telling you—'

Passers-by had stopped to listen to his ranting, but now they scurried off. Savage felt isolated, in the open, without cover – an easy target – and it occurred to him he'd been set up. The two of them, alone, in the now deserted square. His scalp tingled, warning him and he was moving when the first shot came.

He felt a stabbing pain as a slug carried his hat away and creased his scalp. The second came as he dived sideways.

It seemed that his head exploded into an expanding ball of white light, blinding him, and then he was falling out of control. He somehow missed the ground and went on falling into a grey featureless pit and continued falling . . .

. . . Jim Doyle started running as soon as he heard the first shot. He'd been taken by surprise, despite following Savage at a discreet distance, and was disgusted with himself.

When the second shot echoed and people scattered, he spotted a rifle muzzle high up in the clock tower, and swore. By that time Savage was down and Doyle was torn between the need to help him and a violent urge to go after the rifleman.

The cripple hobbled from the square and, still muttering beneath his breath, Doyle knelt beside the unmoving body. The shooter, and he could guess who it was, would have to wait.

Savage's hat had gone and his head and face smeared with blood. He felt for a pulse and found one, erratic and weak, but still a pulse.

'Will someone help me get this man to Doc's?' he shouted.

One man stepped up, but not to help. Gruber thrust a hand into Savage's shirt pocket and pulled out a five-dollar bill.

'He won't be earning that,' he said, and walked off. Doyle glared after him. Nobody offered to help and he couldn't see how he would manage on his own. Hell, Savage looked hardly more than a kid, and a small one at that, sprawled on the ground.

He was feeling desperate when a quiet sing-song voice said, 'I shall help you, Mr Doyle.'

He looked round to see Ma Hubbard's partner, and nodded acceptance. 'You take his feet, J.C.'

Doyle got his hands under Savage's shoulders and lifted. He discovered the skinny Chinese was stronger and faster than he looked. Together they carried the inert body on to the sidewalk, arms dangling, and along to the church hall that doubled as a hospital.

This was a large wooden building, partitioned into rooms. Someone had already alerted Dr Perry and he was waiting with a nurse.

'On the table, please. Tulip, a pillow – I want his head raised slightly. Wash the blood away.'

Despite her size, the black woman obeyed with swift, smooth movements, trimming the straw-coloured hair back with a pair of scissors to expose the wound.

The doctor bent over to peer closely, then gently probed where a bullet had ploughed a furrow. He hummed softly to himself, setting Doyle's teeth on edge.

'Hmm, shallow, and it seems clean . . . touched the brain in one place. Antiseptic, Tulip.'

She brought a small bottle and a swab and he dabbed it on.

'No reaction. All right, Tulip, bandage his head and let's get him to bed. Add an extra blanket for warmth.'

She lifted Savage as easily as she would a child, laid him on a mattress and removed his boots and loosened his clothing. She pulled the Bowie from its sheath and Doyle took it.

She covered the body with two blankets and moistened his lips with a wet cloth. His breathing was faint. Watching this woman, her skin black as coal, Doyle felt useless.

Savage had been a loner, he realized, sufficient to himself; and now he lay helpless and vulnerable. He asked, 'Will he recover, Doc?'

'Maybe yes, maybe no.' Perry wiped his hands on a towel. 'Head wounds are still something of a mystery, but he's young and strong and so he has as good a chance as anybody.'

'At the moment he's in a coma. He may come out of it, he may not. I can't forecast the future.' He hummed a catchy tune and Doyle strained to hear as he murmured words to it:

'Patients come and patients go, but death goes on for ever.'

Chaney sat at his desk, writing on a large sheet of white paper in capital letters:

FOWLER WILL LOOT PUBLIC FUNDS
Stop this man!
The gambling hall known as
The Wheel of Fortune
holds IOUs to the value of
ten thousand dollars
signed by Mr Fowler
Don't trust this man with your money
Make him pay his own debts!
VOTE CHANEY

Gruber, standing before the desk, watched admiringly. He could read, slowly, but writing defeated him. And Chaney's pen moved as if he'd been a scribe all his life.

'That should fix him, boss. Nobody's going to vote for him after that.' He hesitated. 'Is it true?'

'True? What does that mean? Do you believe voters care? It's what they want to believe that matters.'

Chaney folded the sheet and sealed it.

'Ruining the character of your opponent is what this is about – and the bigger the lie the better. Voters will believe anything of a politician!'

He handed the paper to Gruber.

'Get one of your more reliable men to ride to San Francisco with this and find a printer to run off a hundred or more copies. Tell him to distribute them where the largest number of people will see them.'

Gruber smirked. 'You bet, boss!'

# CHAPTER 5

## THE PRISONER

He was aware he had stopped falling. There was something solid beneath his back, but the grey mist persisted. It was quiet, but small sounds crept through the silence. He had no idea where he was until his nose detected a smell of antiseptic.

The smell brought some memory cells back to life: a rifle shot, a stunning blow to the head, falling . . .

A feeling of relief swept through him: he was alive. The relief faded when he tried to move and failed; it seemed he had lost control of his muscles. He tried to call out but no sound came from his throat. Panic was close when he heard breathing and realized someone was nearby.

Pale silvery light flooded from a high window: moonlight. It was night time and that accounted for the grey gloom and the quiet. He was in a bed, but not in his room at Ma Hubbard's.

He tried again to move, an arm, a leg, even a finger; nothing happened. He must be paralysed, just lying there, helpless. A wave of fear surged through him and then pain swamped that. His head hurt . . .

A dark figure loomed over him. A comforting voice sounded.

'Relax, young man, just take it easy now. You're safe here, and in good hands.'

A damp cloth moistened his lips. 'I'll change your dressing now.'

He heard the scratch of a match striking; the flare of an oil lamp filled the room before the wick was adjusted. He saw a large woman in a starched white uniform; a nurse. Her dusky skin and woman-scent roused him. She placed a hand on his thigh and chuckled.

'Oh, oh! This one's alive. Tulip knows when a man patient has decided to live!'

Massive, but delicate hands unwound the bandages about his head; a pad was removed, allowing cool night air to circulate. She brought warm water and sponged the wound, applying fresh anti-septic.

'Yep, sure is healthy looking. Doctor will be pleased.' She put a fresh pad in place and wound a new bandage around his head. 'You sleep good now.'

The lamp was turned down and he stared into the dark. He'd seen no other beds, and he was alone once the nurse left. It was nice to know he was being cared for . . . but as the hours passed he felt cut off. Still unable to move or speak. Isolated. A prisoner in his own skull.

East of Sacramento the road climbed into foothills and, at one point, crossed a railroad track. A heavy locomotive, hauling bullion from the mines in the mountains travelled at speed on the downhill run, and so nobody gave serious thought to a hold-up at that point.

Except Max Chaney. As a shareholder he had access to information about the gold train, the day and the time it ran. It was obvious he wasn't going to rob himself.

Gruber, the gang leader, nursed a secret admiration for Chaney; the politician had a brain and used it. He knew what he wanted and went straight for it. Only afterwards would it be clear that he'd have all the bullion and not just a share.

Gruber had finally caught on that Chaney didn't seek wealth; he needed money to finance his bid to be elected governor. They said money could buy anything, but Chaney said it could buy anyone.

Gruber wasn't clever, but he could understand that. He had a natural cunning and figured he could get whatever he wanted by clinging to Chaney's coat-tails. As the boss went up in the world, so would he. After all, every politician needed somebody to do the dirty work while he paraded an innocent front in public.

Standing beside the crossing, Gruber sucked on a cheroot as he surveyed the set-up.

The new man, Ike, straddled the iron rails with a horse and wagon, apparently in difficulties. His regular crew were under whatever cover was handy to the track; bushes, outcrops of rock, a stunted tree. The horses were well back and screened by a bunch of oaks. The whole area looked innocent enough.

Gruber bent over the rails, listening, then straightened up and made a circular movement with his arm to indicate a train was coming.

He dropped his cheroot and ground it out with a boot heel, then moved to the cover he'd already chosen and dropped flat. He watched Ike, on the rails, hauling at the horse's reins as the wagon refused to budge; the brake had been securely lashed so the rear wheels couldn't turn.

The locomotive came down the slope ahead of the bullion coach; in the cab, the engineer had a view ahead as the train rushed headlong towards the obstruction. Ike dropped the reins and leapt to safety.

'Too early,' Gruber muttered, and frowned.

The engineer saw the horse struggling to get free, and applied the brake in time, slowing as the animal reared up, neighing shrilly.

The locomotive stopped a few yards short and the apelike Gruber, now masked, sprang upright gripping a revolver.

His men swarmed about the stationary train.

Smelly leapt into the locomotive's cab, waving a knife large enough to take off a man's head and shouting, 'Douse the fire!'

Gunshots from further back proved that the bullion coach carried armed guards and that they intended to make a fight of it. Gruber smiled, knowing they were out-numbered.

'Get the wagon free and ready to load up,' he told Ike and waddled back to the bullion coach. Masked men surrounded it.

'Cease fire,' he shouted. 'Reload. When I give the word, all shoot at once. Pour the lead in and aim low.' He waited till they were ready. 'Now!'

A fusillade of slugs hammered the coach and, eventually, one of the guards was hit and cried out.

Gruber signalled his men to stop firing. 'Come out with your hands up and I'll spare you,' he called. 'Chuck your guns out first.'

'Damn you!' There was a pause, then the door opened a fraction. 'Can we trust you?'

'It's the gold we want. Not you.'

The door was pushed wide, rifles and revolvers dropped outside. One guard helped the wounded man to the ground.

'Watch them,' Gruber said.

Ike brought up the horse and wagon and men started to unload gold bars from the coach and load them aboard the wagon, watched in a glum silence by the train crew and guards. They were not going to be popular when, finally, they reached Sacramento.

Gruber prowled up and down, long arms swinging. The wagon began to sag under the weight of bullion. 'Enough,' he said. 'Get going.'

They brought their horses out of hiding and mounted.

Ike looked back longingly at the gold bars left behind. 'We could carry one each, two even.'

'And what would you do with it? Apart from the weight slowing you down, try to sell it and everyone would know who robbed the train.'

They moved off, riders protectively surrounding the wagon. They stuck to the road till they were out of sight of the train crew, then removed their masks and followed an animal track into the hills.

Ike had a broad smile. 'So easy . . . we could just keep going with the gold, share it out and disappear. There's enough here to make every one of us rich.'

Gruber lit a cheroot and gave him a long stare. 'You crazy? How long would it take the boss to find yuh? I wouldn't want to be in your boots then.'

Further on, the track narrowed and passed between rock walls. Gruber blew a feather of smoke, and nodded, 'You know what to do, Killy.'

One rider dropped back. The gold convoy went on, with Gruber at the rear, listening. Presently he heard the sound of blasting and falling rock and relaxed. There would be no early pursuit now.

Savage fought to remain calm. He knew he was in one room of a small hospital. From time to time he heard a racking cough from a patient not that far away. He'd learnt the name of the doctor: Perry. He knew the black nurse was called Tulip . . . but he was still paralysed, unable to move or speak.

And this terrified him. Never in his life had he lacked some control of his situation, no matter how bad. He couldn't ask for help or lift a finger to protect himself. If the shooter came back to finish the job he was helpless.

Worse, he had no idea when he might recover. 'Coma' was the word the doctor used, and refused to commit himself beyond that. He dared not believe he might not come out of it. Of course he would. He had to.

He considered the rifleman: Boyd? Who else could it be? And promised himself satisfaction when he recovered. When . . . if . . .

With the coming of daylight, he studied the ceiling. There were cracks, discoloured patches, cobwebs. A little imagination produced faces from the past, the map of a landscape, anything he chose to see.

He watched a spider at a fly stuck in its web, and thought of himself caught in Chaney's web. Again he tried to move a finger, a toe, an eyelid. He failed. He tried to speak, and failed again.

Tulip bustled in with a steaming bowl and spoon-fed him soup. 'We've got to keep your strength up,' she murmured. A caring person, but she had other patients to attend to. Dr Perry inspected his wound and declared himself satisfied.

The hours passed slowly and evening came again. The temperature dropped and Tulip laid another blanket over him. He waited for the moon to show at the window and travel across the sky, listened to the night sounds. A feeling of desperation threatened to overwhelm him.

He tried to quieten his fears but, as the dark dragged on, hope began to fade.

Max Chaney was waiting downstairs for the hold-up gang to return. His twisted leg was hurting and he kept pacing, leaning on his stick. They should have been back before this. Sacramento was already buzzing with news of the robbery.

The door was pushed open and, one by one, the gang straggled in. Even Gruber looked weary; his men obviously were in no mood to be called to an accounting, even though the business had taken longer than expected.

Chaney suppressed his impatience and kept his voice low and controlled. 'How did it go?'

'Well enough. We delivered the load to the back door at Ward's.'

For a moment, Gruber thought he saw an expression of relief cross Chaney's face. Get it over with, he thought, and pushed Ike forward.

'One small problem. Our new man was all for dividing the loot on the spot and taking off.'

'Was he?' Chaney's face suddenly became a mask

of such chilling fury that Ike took a step backwards.

'A joke,' he muttered. 'That's all!'

'You regard my political future as a joke . . .'

The words came out in a hissing sound. Chaney cast aside his stick. He seemed to straighten and grow tall; his arms shot out and his hands curled around Ike's neck and tightened.

Chaney lifted him without apparent effort so Ike's toes left the floor, his legs kicked uselessly and his face changed colour as he began to choke.

Chaney's grip tightened and the other members of the gang watched in silence.

Gruber raised the trapdoor, pleased the boss had demonstrated he was more than just a brain, that he still had the ability to scare the toughest of them.

Chaney dropped the body into the hole and it fell into the river and sank, to be carried away by the current.

Gruber lowered the trapdoor. He saw a momentary gleam of satisfaction on the face of Max Chaney, a glow that comes only from direct physical action.

# CHAPTER 6

## THE CIRCUS

With the sunrise Savage didn't feel quite so down. There were sounds of life again, a patient coughing, someone arguing, people bustling about. He told himself there was a good chance he'd recover, it was only a matter of time ... changed that to, he *would* recover. He struggled to move, to speak, but achieved nothing.

He detected a general air of excitement but couldn't work out what was happening. Dr Perry inspected his wound again and pronounced himself satisfied. Tulip re-bandaged his head, moistened his lips and helped him use a bed pan.

They left together, discussing other patients and he told himself, they're busy people, but still he felt neglected. He was beginning to feel sorry for himself when Ma Hubbard arrived.

'There you are! I'm not sure I need a boarder who gets himself shot as soon as my back's turned, but Mr Doyle seems to think you're worth saving and Tulip needs some time off.'

She began to spoonfeed him, talking all the while.

'You won't have heard, shut away here, but there's been a robbery. The gold train was held up by masked men and rumours are flying like bats at sunset.

'And it seems that awful man Chaney threatened Fred's daughter, so our dude cowboy has rushed off to guard her.'

This appeared to amuse Ma.

'I suspect Mr Doyle fancies young Alice – and why not? – or he'd be in to see you himself. You don't want to get the idea we're all scared of Chaney, but it pays to be careful. You weren't careful enough, and that's a fact.'

She rambled on and, when she finally left, Savage was seriously disturbed because now he had to depend on other people; and that was something he was not used to.


Max Chaney stood by the window, looking down at two men pasting posters to a wall. He reached behind him for a ship's telescope and focused: words leapt to his eye.

VOTE FOWLER
*The People's Choice*

A police officer stood watching and doing nothing to stop them. A frown creased Chaney's face. People were so stupid; it seemed he had to continually oversee some men to enforce his orders.

He picked up his stick; with its help he could move quickly despite his lurching gait. Downstairs, he called to Gruber, 'Come.'

'What is it, boss?'

He didn't bother to answer. Gruber exchanged a look with Boyd and followed.

Chaney headed for the bill-stickers. 'Officer!' He spoke sharply and the policeman swung round.

'Yes, sir?'

'I'm sure you know the back entrance of the Nugget. There is a private room set aside where you can drink at no expense to yourself. You know it? Good! Take yourself there now . . . Gruber!'

Chaney motioned at the men with paste brushes.

'I get yuh, boss. This pair have to learn to fall in line, yes?'

'Yes.'

The apeman waddled forward, eyes gleaming. Sleeves rolled up, hairs bristled on the corded muscles of his forearms. He grabbed the nearest man and slammed him against the wall and said, 'Tear it down.'

After he'd got his breath back, Fowler's man said, 'I won't, and you can't make me!'

Gruber's face split in a wide grin. He lit a cheroot and blew on it till the end glowed. 'Smoke?'

'No, I—'

As Gruber jabbed the burning weed into his eye, the bill-paster screamed and clutched his face. Gruber balled a rock-hard hand and drove it into his stomach. The man went down, hugging himself, tears streaming from his damaged eye.

Gruber stamped on him with a metal-shod boot and turned to the second man. 'You tear it down.'

White-faced, this one obeyed.

'You see? A lesson learned, and you won't do it again, will you?'

'Never!'

Chaney viewed his collapse with approval. He watched the man on the ground, blubbering as he tried to crawl away. He admired Gruber's direct approach to discipline, enjoyed the feeling of power that another's fear gave him.

A shadow fell across his face. Someone had stepped into the room and stood silently watching him. Savage's skin crawled and he cursed his immobility; he couldn't even turn his head to see who it was. For a moment he thought it might be Chaney's redheaded gunman come to finish the job.

One quiet step forward and a figure loomed above him. A stranger, but in some way familiar, wearing a dark suit. The visitor didn't speak, just stared down with a calculating eye. He reminded Savage of a vulture waiting for its prey to die.

The stranger began to whistle softly, a tune Savage

had heard before; a tune Dr Perry often hummed. Then the doctor appeared behind him and Savage could see a similarity.

'What are you doing here, Richard? Are you mocking me?'

'Of course not, Bro. But it is a catchy little tune – "Patients come, and patients go, but death goes on for ever" – and something I heartily agree with. You do realize you're famous, of course? While I'm measuring up, does this one have the price of a coffin?'

'He's not dead yet. And he won't die if I can do anything for him.'

'A noble ideal, but can you? How many of your mistakes have I buried, Bro?'

'I thought Chaney's gang kept you busy.'

'True.' Richard Perry rubbed his fingers together as if counting banknotes. 'And, do you know, Mr Chaney pays my bills promptly and without questioning expenses?'

'Glad to have the evidence buried and forgotten, no doubt!'

They're talking as if I'm not here, Savage thought. Do they think I can't hear?

'I trust you not to relay news of this patient's survival to Chaney, Richard.'

The undertaker shrugged. 'Why would I need to do that, Bro? It seems to be common knowledge already – after all, a coma is not the usual result of a gunshot!'

*

Olsen sighed. This job was taking far too long and Chaney wouldn't be pleased. Even with the help of a clerk from City Hall, these idiots – if they could read or write at all – had peculiar ideas about spelling.

Worse, some were superstitious. Hard men who wouldn't hesitate to murder a lawman were visibly nervous about being in a graveyard. They stuck close together, were reluctant to go near shadowy undergrowth, and kept looking over their shoulders.

And this job exposed him. It made him conspicuous, a situation he normally shunned. He prided himself on being Mr Average, his features plain, his clothes a neutral grey. He made a habit of being overlooked, ignored, a mere shadow of a man.

As a dedicated craftsman – penman and forger – he operated best in a cellar by artificial light, quietly forgotten. But Chaney had picked him for this job and he was a dangerous man to refuse.

So he toiled in sunlight, supervising Gruber's men and drifters who needed drinking money as they crawled among the tombstones, copying names to provide extra votes at the polling booth.

It was an old cemetery and neglected, overgrown by brambles and nettles, and Olsen wore gloves to protect his hands.

It amused him to see these roughnecks backing away from a swarm of mosquitoes, or cursing as a thorn ripped their flesh.

There was one man who smelled so bad the others avoided him. Olsen kept well away which was lucky because Smelly disturbed a nest of wasps and panicked. He turned and ran, pursued by an angry horde of insects.

Olsen allowed himself a rare smile as Gruber's bunch gave a rousing cheer.

The sound of music alerted Savage to the outside world again. Trapped inside his head he was starting to forget that anything else existed.

Tulip had attended to him, and gone. No visitors came; he watched a bare wall and a shadow-shape as the sun moved slowly across the sky.

Music was a new experience here, and gave him a welcome lift. It was cheerful music played with gusto by a brass band; something was going on in that other world of which he was no longer a part.

He heard cheering, and laughter, and the excited shouts of youngsters; the clip-clop of horses' hoofs and the trundling of heavy wheels. A procession?

It was only when he heard and smelled the animals that he guessed a circus had come to town, and recalled a poster he'd seen when he first arrived in Sacramento.

But unless he came out of his coma he was going to miss the show, except in his imagination. And he could imagine the bareback riders, the jugglers and the trained animals; as the music now blared into the *Entry of the Gladiators*, imagination merged with memory then and he was stepping over guy ropes, lifting canvas to wriggle into a big top in New York when he was a boy. . . .

. . . inside was such a world he'd never dreamed existed, a world of colour and daring and exotic animals. He was held enchanted by a girl in spangles standing on the back of a horse circling the sawdust ring. He held his breath when an acrobat released his hold on a swinging trapeze and soared through space to grip the hands of the catcher on another trapeze. His pulse rate jumped when a man with a chair opened the door of a cage containing lions and stepped inside and the door was bolted on the outside after him. He thrilled at the sheer bulk and size of an elephant and laughed till his ribs ached at the antics of the clowns.

But all this was a prelude to the act which sparked an enthusiasm to imitate.

Roustabouts carried a table into the ring; they set up a large wooden board in a vertical position. A blonde girl with a full figure appeared and stood in front of the board, a glittering goddess under the floodlights.

'Ladies and gentlemen,' the ringmaster announced, after a fanfare by trumpets. 'For the next act, I must ask you to keep perfectly still and quiet. Any distraction is likely to result in the disfigurement or death of this young lady.' She gave a little wave to the audience. 'For your entertainment. I give you . . . Tonio and Tania!'

A swarthy man dressed Mexican-style strode into the ring with two handfuls of knives which he placed in order on the table. He took measured paces from the board and marked the ground with a tape.

Tania stood motionless, her back against the board. To a drum roll, Tonio picked up a knife, tried it for balance and toed his mark. He aimed and threw and the knife stuck in the board close to her head. He threw a second and a third while the crowd waited in silence for him to miss and hit the girl.

But every throw of his knives ended up close but just missing her. He worked his way down each side of her body, from head to feet; when he threw the last knife, she stepped away to reveal her outline in knives stuck in the board.

Savage, held spellbound, let out his breath and gulped in air. The performers turned to face their audience, hand in hand, bowing and smiling. Then they ran out of the ring together.

Savage, living rough on the dockside, knew about knife-fighting, but this kind of throwing came close to art and he was awed. Next morning, early, he was back at the circus, watching the artistes practise or rehearse new acts for the show.

A juggler worked with flaming torches; a man with an umbrella took to the high wire; acrobats limbered up; clowns worked up a new routine; a man in overalls fed the lions raw meat.

But the one he looked for was Tonio; the knife-thrower set up a target and Savage watched closely as the Mexican picked up each knife in turn, tested it for balance and aimed. He hit the bull each time.

Tonio saw him edging nearer and paused. 'You like the knife, yes? You want to try?'

Savage nodded eagerly. Tonio retrieved his knives and handed one to him. 'Let's see what you can do.' Savage weighed the knife in his hand, aimed and threw. He came close to the centre.

'Not bad, keed.' Tonio selected another. 'Test this one for balance . . . shift your grip, so.' He demonstrated his own hold.

Savage drew a steady breath, aimed and threw. He hit the bull.

'Better. Quick to learn too. Keep throwing.'

Tonio watched with approval, nodding. 'I'd guess you're a natural, and so you must keep practising. A professional practises every day.'

The Mexican's words came as a revelation; never before had Savage grasped the importance of regular practice.

# CHAPTER 7

# DOC'S DILEMMA

The Nugget was busy, but not as busy as usual. Men were drinking and talking, a few playing cards at a table away from the bar. One man, hat pushed to the back of his head, contemplated a large picture of a naked woman as reflected in three angled mirrors; he was muttering to himself.

Chaney decided this touring circus would have to pay a hefty tax for taking business away from him. He crossed the L-shaped bar-room, followed by Boyd, and went upstairs to the manager's office.

He regularly and personally checked the books kept by all the managers of the places of business he owned. The threat of instant and lethal dismissal by Boyd kept them honest.

The Nugget's manager stood so Chaney could use his chair and waited to answer questions as his boss ran an eye down columns of figures. He perspired slightly.

A knock at the door interrupted them. Boyd unshipped his revolver and opened the door.

Killy offered a folded and sealed paper. 'Message for the boss. It came just after he left.'

Boyd nodded and said, 'Wait.' He passed the note to Chaney who broke the seal to read: *The herd will arrive tomorrow.*

The message was not unexpected and, coming when it did, offered a solution to another problem. 'Is that Texan still around?'

'Yep,' Boyd replied. 'He's hanging around Hooper's daughter.'

'No doubt.' Chaney had other ideas about the man who'd got Savage to a doctor; his suspicions about the cowboy were growing.

'Killy, bring this Texan to me here. I have a job for him.'

'Sure thing, boss.'

Killy left, and Chaney closed the door and went back to the books he'd been studying; this manager, at least, was too canny to take risks.

He needed an experienced cowhand, and it would get Doyle away from Hooper and Savage. The newspaper editor could be ignored, but the word going around suggested that Savage might recover.

'Boyd, after I see the Texan, tell Killy to bring Dr Perry here.'

\*

Savage listened to rain hammering the roof of the hospital; when it poured off it sounded like a waterfall and drowned out all other sounds.

What sky was visible through the window was a sullen grey, a blanket of low cloud. He felt bored and frustrated. Bored because no visitors braved the deluge to talk to him; frustrated because he could glimpse a discarded newspaper across the room and was unable to lift his body or turn his head to read even the headlines. He supposed Chaney was still electioneering.

He wanted to scream. He wanted to attack somebody. Anybody. Anything rather than lie here in grey gloom listening to the rain come down.

He felt hollow and imagined a thick juicy steak followed by peach pie. Would he ever enjoy food again? A woman? He wondered where the Texan was: still watching Alice?

Jim Doyle, wearing a slicker, was riding a horse up into the hills, following after Chaney's horse-drawn carriage. Chaney and Boyd sat inside, under cover, but he bore the fury of a wind-driven rain-storm. Water dripped from his Stetson and even his horse found the climb a hard one.

By the time they reached a green and soggy plateau where a spread-out herd of longhorns grazed, the rain had stopped and the sun was turning the excess moisture into steam.

The herd was small by Texan standards, but large

enough to keep Sacramento in beef for a month.

The carriage rolled to a halt and the trail boss, a veteran hand, approached. 'You've brought the money?'

Chaney opened the door and passed out a canvas bag. The trail boss regarded it with some suspicion; he was used to selling in a town market, but the bag was stuffed with bundles of banknotes. He checked a few and made a rough count.

'Good enough – the herd's yours. D'yuh want us to drive the critters to any special place?'

Chaney watched the cattle graze; they seemed docile enough, and there was a creek nearby. The view was open and a man could see for a considerable distance. A clump of trees offered shelter.

'No, just leave them. I have a man to watch them.'

The trail boss glanced at Doyle and didn't seem impressed. 'Him?'

'Him,' Chaney agreed.

'Your business.' The veteran waved his men to their horses. 'We're finished here – let's hit the town.'

He tied the money bag to his saddle and rode away.

Doyle looked at his charges. For the moment they appeared content to rest and graze, but he knew that any unexpected noise could send them running.

'You seriously expect one man to hold this lot if they decide to visit the horizon?'

'It's only for a day or two, Mr Doyle, and you'll be well paid for your time. Tomorrow, I'll send you one of Gruber's men – not to herd cattle, but to use as a messenger if you need help.'

Chaney's voice stayed flat, as if he were intoning a law of nature. 'Some of the butchers in town may get the notion they can help themselves to my beef. I expect you to discourage that idea.' He glanced at the Colt hanging at the Texan's hip. 'I suppose you can use that weapon?'

Doyle palmed the revolver, then holstered it again. He stared blankly. 'You're the boss, of course, but what's this about?'

Chaneys face twisted in a smile.

'Until I'm elected governor I shall control the meat market in Sacramento. Nobody eats beef except those I favour. A few selected butchers will sell my meat, at my price, to my supporters. It's a matter of encouraging the waverers to vote for me, Mr Doyle. Now, can I trust you to discourage those who would help themselves?'

Doyle lifted his hat to scratch an itch. 'Yep, I guess you can.'

Chaney stepped back into the carriage and sat opposite Boyd. The driver turned the horses and started down the hill, leaving Jim Doyle alone to nursemaid a herd of steers.

'Yep,' he repeated, 'and while I'm here, what happens to Alice? And Savage?'

*

Savage's notion of time was vague. It could be evening, he supposed. Beyond the window was a grey gloom as he lay motionless, listening intently. Someone, somewhere, was crying.

The rain had stopped or he wouldn't have heard the stifled sobbing. Perhaps a patient had died? Perhaps it was only a broken heart? Whoever it was was trying to be as quiet as possible.

The door opened and closed, but no one spoke. A figure moved across his field of vision, across the room to the medicine cabinet and opened it. Dr Perry.

For once, Savage was startled. Tulip, with the doctor, had taken good care of him, and he wanted to say so, to thank them both, but words were just not possible.

The doctor, crying? After a while, Perry got a grip on himself, opened a bottle and poured liquid into a glass. He approached the bed.

His voice was soft, emotion controlled now. 'Swallow this, Mr Savage. For me, please, just swallow this.'

The glass touched his lips, tilted, then a hand came out of the gloom. 'No, Brother, that's not the way. Allow me.'

The glass was taken away and emptied down the sink. Dr Perry started crying again. 'My family, Richard. He threatened my family—'

'Of course he did. That sums up Mr Chaney – he always knows what will force a man to do what he wants. If I were a religious man I'd call him evil, but he is what he is.'

'He threatened my wife and family if I don't—'

'We all take risks, Bro. What is important is to keep our hands clean. Between us, we shall remove Mr Savage to a place of safety, after dark. I shall leave now to prepare a hiding place.'

Richard Perry looked solemn in a dark suit.

'But my—'

'No buts, Bro. Your story is, while you were away, the patient recovered and walked out.'

'That's not very likely, is it?'

Richard gave a ghost of a smile. 'No more likely than you saving his life, Bro. Warn Tulip to expect a visit once Chaney learns Mr Savage has gone . . . and remember your own words.'

He left as quietly as he'd come. Dr Perry washed his face at the sink, took a deep breath and stepped towards the bed. 'Try to forgive me, Mr Savage. I acted in a moment of weakness.'

Savage would have had a lot to say if he could, but his struggles achieved nothing. Dr Perry left the room, head bowed; and in that moment, Savage decided to forget Allan Pinkerton's orders. He would deal with Max Chaney in his own way, in his own time, when he recovered. If he recovered.

It gave him something to plan while he lay helpless in the gathering dusk. With darkness came a glimmer of oil lamps, and he studied a solitary star in a black sky. The sounds of late-night drinkers gradually faded. Now he could hear the agitated scratching of a small mouse.

In almost perfect silence the door opened and Dr Perry and his brother slipped inside.

'Were moving you, Mr Savage,' the doctor whispered. 'You are no longer safe here.'

Between them, the brothers lifted him, wrapped him in a blanket, placed him on a trolley and wheeled him outside. They waited a moment, in deep shadow, and then trundled him along the boardwalk.

'Suppose we're seen?' the doctor murmured.

'Stop worrying, Bro. It'll be taken for granted I'm just collecting the latest stiff.'

Savage breathed in the cool night air, a pleasant change after the medical smells, until they stopped. He could make out a sign: *The Coffin Shop.*

Richard pushed open a door and wheeled him inside. He lit a lamp and Dr Perry closed the door.

'No trouble you see, Bro. Strangely, few people seem keen to visit me.' He chuckled. 'Help me lift him into this coffin. Everyone expects to see a corpse in a coffin, so let them look all they like.'

The doctor protested. 'He shouldn't be left like this.'

'Probably not, but it won't be for long.'

'He needs care and attention—'

'So he won't be the first to go without! As soon as Tulip's home has been searched by you-know-who, we can move him there.'

Savage wondered how long he'd be in this new home: after the hospital bed, a wooden board felt hard and unyielding. Hiding in a coffin was not something he'd imagined he'd ever have to do.

# CHAPTER 8

# COFFIN CURE

'Today of all days!'

Max Chaney kept his voice low and a scowl off his face as he greeted voters outside the main polling station. But inwardly, fury was stoked to furnace heat as he stood under a banner with the message:

*Free Drinks. Vote Chaney.*

He had been dressed for the occasion by the best tailor in Sacramento and wore a tophat and a hothouse bloom in his buttonhole.

Gruber had just brought the bad news in person; Savage had disappeared. He added, 'We searched that nurse's place. No sign he was ever there. Maybe he did recover and walk.'

'And maybe not.' Chaney kept his voice down,

smiling at the voters he hadn't bought. 'It'll have to wait. Winning this election is the important thing today. Savage will keep.' He glanced at his body-guard. 'Anyway, you're the one who shot him, so it's you he'll be after. Does that worry you?'

Boyd shrugged. Other men had been after him in the past, and he was still here.

'He'll hardly be at his best. Likely he'll go to ground.'

Gruber's men were stopping anyone they suspected of supporting the opposition. Chaney had already suggested to the police officers on duty that they were not needed, giving him effective control of this polling station.

So far, the election seemed to be going well, with his men voting again and again under different names. He noticed Fred Hooper taking notes at a discreet distance, and beckoned to him.

'I trust you're going to give your new governor a good write up in the *Union*? There'll be a barbecue afterwards to celebrate my victory, and all my friends are welcome – you'll find there's no shortage of beef!'

Hooper jotted down a fresh note, his pencil stab-bing the paper, and Chaney smiled. There were times when people were so easy to read.

'By that time, Hooper, I'll be untouchable.'

But still a small niggling doubt crept into his mind: where was Savage?'

*

Savage lay in his coffin, contemplating a different ceiling; this one consisted of planks of wood with some interesting knots. It had warped over time and now had a network of cracks, some filled with mud. The newer ones had shadows that might hide anything.

It was a bare room, the windows painted over so the sunlight was dimmed. His coffin rested on two trestles; a partially glimpsed door led to another room and he could smell freshly sawn wood. At the moment he was feeling abandoned; neither the doctor, nor Tulip, had been near him.

The shop door opened and he heard a woman's voice: 'What d'you charge to bury a child?'

Richard said, 'The same as for anyone else.'

'It should be half-price for a half-size coffin.' Savage couldn't see her, but her voice was sharp.

'I can adjust the price if that's what you want.' Richard sounded pleasantly agreeable. An undertaker with a heart of gold? Savage would have raised an eyebrow if that were possible.

'But, of course, you'll want the best. Seasoned oak that won't rot in the ground, a decent lining—'

'Of course,' she said promptly.

And each little extra would bring the price back up to Richard's original figure. Savage tried again to move an arm, a leg, and had no more success than before.

The woman left and he could hear people passing by outside; there seemed to be more than usual, drunken shouting, music. Another parade? Later, he heard Gruber speaking.

'Now, sir, you are going to vote, aren't you? If you'll agree to support Mr Chaney, there need be no unpleasantness at all.'

It's today, Savage realized, the election is today – and he was supposed to have stopped Chaney. Knowledge of his failure depressed him and he began to talk to himself, silently.

What would happen to him now? Did anyone know where he was, or care? Where was Doyle when he needed him ... needed? He'd never needed anyone before! Would Mr Allan investigate? Locked inside his head, he began to feel increasingly sorry for himself.

Then Richard Perry stepped alongside the coffin and said quietly, 'I'm closing the lid now, but don't worry, I bored air holes in the side. We'll be on our way while Chaney is distracted by the election.'

The lid came down and immediately he was in darkness. He heard the undertaker's voice, muffled, 'Take the front end, Jack.'

He felt himself lifted. The coffin swayed, levelled again and was carried forward; he slid into the hearse. After a pause, a whip cracked and horses strained to get the wheels moving.

The hearse kept to the centre of the main thoroughfare and noisy supporters paused in their arguing with rival voters.

Savage found himself jerked about as the wheels of

the hearse stuck in muddy ruts. It was some time before the horses settled to a steady funereal gait.

Then a few of the crowd removed their hats to hold against their hearts as the cortège passed. A majority probably had more interest in the dead than who might win the election.

In his coffin, Savage realized he had no idea where Tulip lived. They could just as easily take him to a cemetery where an open grave waited to receive him. Suppose they buried his wooden box and filled in the grave before he came out of his coma?

He grew acutely aware of the few small air holes supplying him. The air was already stuffy. He sweated, realizing again that he had to trust other people, and his whole life had been spent trusting no one.

As he jolted from one mudhole to the next, fear gnawed like a rat, tormenting him, and he remembered a story he'd read in a newspaper years ago.

In this story, and he hoped the author had made it up, the victim came back to life after he'd been buried. It told, in terrifying detail, how he'd clawed at the surrounding woodwork, breaking his fingernails, pummelled the screwed-down lid with clenched hands and screamed until he used up his limited supply of air.

The memory of the story tortured his imagination until the hearse lurched suddenly, bringing him back to his present confinement. It had left the road and was bumping its way over loose planks set in the mud.

The noise of the crowd faded and the journey ended.

Richard's helper asked, 'Why are we stopping here?'

'Never mind why. Give me a hand to unload the coffin and keep your mouth shut. I've told you before, in this job we never talk about a client.'

Savage felt himself lifted, heard Tulip's voice, 'In here,' and his momentary fear lifted. The coffin bumped against a door frame and – 'Careful!' – one end crashed down, banging his head with bruising force.

'Sorry,' Jack mumbled, 'it slipped.'

For several seconds, Savage seemed to be standing on his head in pitch dark. Half-stunned, tears came to his eyes, then the coffin was level again.

'Get him out and on to the bed,' Tulip said.

The lid was raised and daylight dazzled him: he closed his eyes. He was moved on to something soft enough to give way under him.

Jack sounded puzzled. 'What's going on here?'

'Nothing's going on,' Richard Perry answered shortly. 'You've seen nothing. You say nothing.'

Cautiously, Savage half-opened his eyes to see where he was.

The cabin was small with a curtain across the window and flowers in a jug; there was a rug on the floor and he could smell polish. Through the open door he glimpsed a back alley.

Richard closed the coffin and, with Jack helping, carried it outside; the hearse moved off and Tulip closed the door.

She bent over him. 'Let's have a look at your head.'

Belatedly, Savage realized he'd closed his eyes and opened them again. Excited, because he had some control back, he tried to move his right hand and the fingers obeyed. He croaked, 'I'm hungry.'

'How like a man, always thinking of his stomach . . . *Oh!*'

Tulip hurried to bring him a mug of water to ease his throat. 'Food,' he said.

'You took a nasty bump on the head—'

'That can wait. My stomach's growling. I need something solid, one beefsteak at least.'

'The doctor ought to see you.'

'Later,' Savage insisted. 'I need real food to get my strength back. That comes first. I'm tired of lying helpless.'

Tulip sighed, but accepted his decision and hurried outside.

When she returned, within a few minutes, with a large dish filled with barbecued beef, she was smiling.

'Courtesy of Chaney. The celebration has started early.'

Savage ate like a starving man, gnawing the meat off the bone and swallowing chunks whole, blood running down his chin; he could feel the strength flowing into him. He slowed down, clearing the dish. Now he could move again, defend himself if necessary.

Satisfied, he allowed Tulip to wash his head and rebandage it. 'Though I doubt the doctor will approve of dropping a patient on his head to cure him!'

Loud cheering and drunken shouting swelled from the direction of City Hall. Above the roar of the crowd, a loudhailer boomed:

'We have a result – Mr Chaney is the new governor!'

# CHAPTER 9

## MANHUNT

The new governor was abroad early next morning. His carriage stopped outside police headquarters and he lurched up the steps, on his stick, followed by his bodyguard.

He was a happy man – the first rung reached on his ladder to power though his expression remained chill and his voice flat.

In the reception area, he said, 'The Chief is expecting me.'

'Yes sir, this way.'

The door at the end of a short passage carried the notice:

CHIEF OF POLICE
*F.A. Anderson.*

Anderson was in uniform, a solid man with a bull neck and hair touched with grey. He didn't rise from his chair.

He nodded. 'Sit down, Chaney. I think we understand each other, so I'll skip the congratulations.' He ignored Boyd; to a policeman, he was just another gunman.

Chaney's face moved in a semblance of a smile; both men put self-interest first. 'But you're as high as you'll ever go.'

'This position suits me. I wonder about you, though. Can you take advice?'

'Try me.'

'Disassociate yourself from the gangs. You can still use them, but through an intermediary, not directly. You'll be under a microscope from now on, and it won't only be Hooper's *Union* asking the questions. And I suggest you move to a hotel till you make more suitable arrangements.'

Chaney nodded. 'I suppose that makes sense, but I called on another matter. Gruber's men have failed to find Savage. I want your men to look for him.'

'We can find him – you do your own killing.'

'Agreed.'

Anderson rose, opened the door and shouted, 'Lew.'

The man who answered the call was small and slight, with a sharply pointed nose and keen gaze. He viewed Chaney with mild interest.

'What is it, Chief?' His voice was quiet, almost a

whisper, and he dressed more like one of Gruber's gang than a police officer. Chaney imagined he could mix easily with men outside the law.

Anderson said, 'Lew is my ferret. I put him down a hole and he flushes out my quarry. Your quarry in this case. He could also act as a go-between for you in any future dealings with Gruber.'

To Lew, he said, 'Chaney wants Savage. D'you know him?'

'Surely. The story goes that Boyd didn't quite finish him, and now he's walked.'

'And Gruber can't find him,' Chaney added.

'Interesting.' Lew turned to the bodyguard. 'I heard you used a cripple to set him up. That right?'

Boyd nodded.

'So what I suggest is' – Lew's voice took on an authoritative quality – 'Something happens to the cripple and I'll find a couple of witnesses to swear it was Savage. Then we can get an official manhunt going, and that'll soon turn him up.'

'I like it,' Chaney said. 'And if a few men get carried away and lynch him, we can turn a blind eye. It'll save the state money.'


Savage moved cautiously, not sure his legs would carry him far. His limbs felt stiff and the joints reluctant to work. He still lacked his full strength; maybe that was why he failed to repulse Tulip's advances last night.

He was alone again. This morning, after she'd

washed his head wound and rebandaged it, she left for the hospital. The curtains were drawn across the window and her last command had been, 'Stay out of sight.'

He had to agree that made sense. His head still ached and he was in no shape to take on Chaney, Boyd and Gruber's gang.

But he was able to move, to speak; he'd been given a new lease on life and that was wonderful. Tulip had been wonderful too.

Her cabin had one room and one bed, which they'd shared, and it soon became obvious she had in mind what comes naturally. She insisted – speaking from her experience as a nurse – that recovery came quicker after a male patient proved he was still a man. He didn't need a lot of convincing, and she seemed intent to prove that a little loving did a lot of good. It was also exhausting.

Savage figured she had it right, even if he was weak as a newborn. Exercise, she told him, work one muscle against another. So he continued to rest, to exercise – push, pull: push, pull – and work up an appetite and anticipate Tulip returning this evening.

And think about Chaney and the need to get some kind of weapon.

Max Chaney stood, alone, in front of a mirror in the best room of the best hotel in Sacramento. Boyd had the room next to his and there was an interconnecting door.

It was disturbing that he looked older than he felt; there were lines he hadn't noticed before, a few grey hairs. It seemed the years of struggle had taken a toll, but he'd kept busy and ignored the signs.

His skin was turning sallow, reminding him how long a fight it had been to bootstrap his way up from the past.

Anderson was right, he admitted. He needed to change the way people saw him. He'd done it once; he could do it again. As governor he would be expected to dress for social occasions, to live in a mansion, to cultivate people who could help him further up the ladder. As the chief had pointed out, he needed to be more discreet about the methods he used to succeed.

Life was all about power. The word excited him, and his face struggled into a smile. He needed to practise smiling, he realized, smiling and bowing. Success was within his grasp: the Senate, then. . . .

He needed to think clearly, to plan ahead. Power: the idea intoxicated him. There was nothing like it; to have life and death control of people excited him. The need for power drove him: to gain it, use it and keep it.

He'd learned his lesson the hard way. He knew, better than most, what it meant to be powerless, in the grip of a bully who despised him. He didn't like to think about the past; that still had the ability to terrify, to drive him to any excess to avoid a repetition. When, in a nightmare, he relived the deep south as a boy, he shuddered . . .

. . . The stagecoach slowed to a halt and the driver called down, 'This here's your stop, boy.'

Max opened the door and jumped down, gripping his haversack. The air was soggy with humidity; it was like trying to breathe warm water. Before, he'd known only the dry dusty heat of the plains.

He was thin and hungry, small for his age. He didn't feel good but that, he knew, was an after-effect of the sickness that had killed his parents and almost finished him.

The driver cracked his whip above the heads of the horses and, reluctantly, they stepped forward. The stage moved off and Max watched till it was out of sight.

Max dropped his haversack and stared about him. He was in a lonely place; an empty place of sickly green vegetation and mud, flies and bird calls. The air hung still as a wet blanket and the river he glimpsed between broad leaves made hardly a sound. Its surface appeared to be thick with weed, the current sluggish; judging by the smell, something had recently died close by.

He began to wonder if he'd come to the right place, and didn't much care. He felt that life had come to an end.

Then he heard the splash of a paddle, water dripping, and moments later a big Negro pushed through the screen of leaves. He wore faded overalls and a straw hat and white teeth dazzled in a face as black as coal.

'You'll be Max Chaney, I guess?'

'Yes. Are you from Uncle Dickon?'

'That's so. You call me Jubilee. Step along with me, Max.'

Max picked up his haversack and followed the big man along an animal track to the water's edge, where a small boat was tied up. He got in the boat after Jubilee and sat down.

Jubilee untied and used a paddle to push off from the bank. He got the boat moving with little apparent effort and Max saw muscles rippling with every stroke. They reached the middle of the river and headed upstream.

The river merged with swampland in places, when Jubilee exchanged the paddle for a long pole. Strange grey trees, low in the water and twisted, blocked any view of the land; their roots sprawled like weed-covered snakes. Mosquitoes swarmed, and Max found himself wiping flies and sweat from his bare flesh. He trailed a hand in the water.

Jubilee frowned. 'No, Max, you can lose a hand that way. There's 'gators here big enough to snatch any tasty snack you offer them.'

Max's eyes opened wide and he quickly jerked his hand out of the water. 'Is it far to Uncle Dickon's?'

'Not that far. Be patient.' Jubilee laid down the pole and took up the paddle again.

Where the river was clear, the boat shot forward; it slowed to a crawl where the weed grew thickest. Max saw no sign of life among the leaves, broad as the blade of a paddle, and tangled vines.

'Why does Uncle Dickon live here?'

'His business is here, Max. You wait and see for yourself.'

Minutes later, Jubilee guided the boat towards the bank where a landing stage had been carved out of the forest. Behind the stage was a wooden house, low and almost hidden among the trees growing around it.

Jubilee cast a rope around a mooring post and helped Max ashore as a man came through the doorway. 'Any trouble, Jubilee?'

'No, sah, no trouble. I brought you Max.'

'Anyone see you collect him?'

'No sah, I wait till the stage leaves. Nobody about at all.'

Max was disturbed by this exchange and looked uneasily at his uncle. He dressed the same as Jubilee, coverall and straw hat and boots; older than Max's parents, he'd let his hair grow long. His whiskers resembled a bristle brush and he carried a long rifle.

'Did you travel alone, Max?'

'Yes, sir.'

'Empty your haversack so I can see what you've brought with you.'

Reluctantly, Max obeyed. He was not sure he liked this uncle, but he was the only family he had. He had few possessions: a knife and a tin mug, a spare shirt, socks and the family Bible.

Dickon snatched at the Bible and studied the list of names crossed through, and smiled. 'Sure looks like you're alone in the world.'

'Except for you. I'm grateful—'

Max broke off, astonished, as Dickon tossed the Bible into the water. It sank slowly as it became water-logged.

'I don't hold with preachers. I make my own damn rules and number one is: work comes first, before eating. Get him ready, Jubilee.'

The Negro brought a heavy iron chain, put a fetter around Max's ankle and locked it. Max felt alarm. 'Why are you doing this?'

'We don't want you running too far.' Dickon broke off a piece of chewing tobacco and put it in his mouth.

Jubilee led Max to the water's edge. 'You sit quiet and stay still.' He fastened him with another chain around the trunk of a tree, and padlocked that in place. He kept that key himself, the first he returned to Dickon.

Max sat with his legs cramped up; the alternative was to dangle them in the river.

'This won't take long,' Dickon said, and loaded his rifle. 'Afterwards, you can eat.'

'Try not to worry,' Jubilee added, 'Dickon rarely misses.'

# CHAPTER 10

## BAIT

A victory celebration was in full swing when Jim Doyle rode into town. He kept away from the main square where drunks fired off revolvers and used backstreets to reach the *Union* office.

He slowed his mount to a walk as he passed and gave a brief wave. Alice Hooper gave him a brilliant smile that encouraged him to believe she was glad to see him again.

When he reached the livery, the stableman said, 'If you ain't heard, Chaney got in.'

'I guessed.'

He went directly to Ma Hubbard's. 'I'm back, Ma, and hungry for a decent meal.'

'So sit at the table. J.C. and me wondered if we'd ever see you again.'

'So did I. . . .'

Ma bustled about in the kitchen to provide a hotpot of meat and vegetables, and it was growing dark when he sat back to use a tooth-pick. 'That's better. I've been missing your cooking since I went away.'

Ma said, 'That's not all. You missed the election, you missed Mr Savage—'

Doyle came alert. 'Did he recover?'

'That's the story, though no one admits to seeing him. He just disappeared.'

'The doctor—?'

'Is keeping quiet. There are rumours, but nobody knows anything for sure – or if they do, they ain't saying.'

Doyle was thoughtful. He still had Savage's shot-gun and Bowie in his room, and the kid was going to need weapons wherever he was.

'Any ideas, J.C?'

Ma's Chinese partner shrugged. 'Gruber visit nurse, not there, who knows? Friend say he see ghost.'

Only too likely, Doyle decided, and chose to start looking at his last known place of residence; the hospital. He collected Savage's weapons and set off.

Although evening shadows were darkening, the door of the church hall stood open and a light was burning when Doyle walked in. 'Doc? Doc Perry?'

'In here.'

The doctor had a patient on his examination table, bandaging a splint to a leg.

'Jim Doyle, from Texas, remember? I brought in Mr Savage – I've just heard he upped and walked. Is that true?'

Perry concentrated on his patient; he was humming a little tune.

'We suppose that's what happened. He simply wasn't here when Tulip and I arrived one morning. And, before you ask, no, I have no idea where he is.'

Doyle watched the doctor binding the splint; he took his time over the job and didn't look up. He seemed scared and reluctant to talk.

'Waal, if you happen to see him, tell him I've got his shotgun and knife.'

He touched the brim of his Stetson and left. Outside, he decided to visit Tulip; she might know something.

He moved quietly along the boardwalk, taking care to avoid those groups still drinking. Any excuse for a party, he thought, especially when someone else was paying. It was dusk, the air chilly, and he heard the tinkle of a piano from one saloon.

The glow from uncurtained windows made regular pools of light among the shadows and, ahead, he saw someone he recognized: a cripple on two sticks. Doyle wondered where he'd been hiding and quickened his pace, intending to question the man who'd lured Savage into the open.

He paused as another figure loomed out of the twilight, tall and thin. He saw a dagger of red flame and heard the crack of a revolver. The cripple dropped one stick as he fell sideways. Doyle hesitated, then moved forward warily, but the killer blended with the shadows as silently as any ghost.

He bent to stoop over the body and knew there was no hope: a heart shot at close quarters. The cripple had died before he reached the ground.

The night sounds faded as other men gathered about the body. Someone said. 'What are you doing here, cowboy?'

Doyle recognized Gruber's voice and straightened up quickly. 'I heard a shot, and was just checking to see if a doctor was needed.'

He realized the men crowding him were some of Gruber's gang.

'That shotgun you're carrying.' The apeman's eyes gleamed with malice. 'Is that Savage's?'

It would be dangerous to deny it. Doyle shrugged as one of the gang took it from him and handed it to Gruber.

The gang boss opened it to check the loads, pushed off the safety, aimed and fired one barrel into the cripple's body.

'That makes it watertight. Everyone can see he was blasted by Savage's gun.' He looked around the circle of faces. 'Where's our witnesses?'

Two drunks were pushed forward.

'You saw the shooter, right? Who was it?'

'Savage.'

'That's good. How did yuh recognize him?'

'He had a bandage around his head.'

'Good.' Gruber swung around to face Doyle, his voice mocking. 'You got that straight? Keep your nose clean, cowboy!'

Max tried to relax, but it was hard. He didn't understand why he was chained to a tree, but nothing bad had happened to him. Yet. He was starving, so the sooner this was over the better. Cramp forced him to stretch his legs out in front of him, and the weight of the iron shackles submerged his feet below the surface of the river.

Jubilee waited, half-hidden behind giant leaves. Uncle Dickon showed only as the muzzle of his rifle. Neither made a sound.

Max watched the water, wondering, uneasy. The river was sluggish. the colour of coconut matting. He felt hot and sticky, and insects swarmed over his bare flesh as if he were a rare treat.

Jubilee called softly, 'Coming.'

Max tensed, about to learn what this was about. Nothing changed. Then he saw a log break surface. Bulging eyes studied him, a broad snout lifted, dripping water. It was coming for him with scarcely a ripple and its mouth opened to reveal overlapping rows of teeth.

Alligator! The shock sent a shudder through him, and he tried to jerk his legs up from the water, but the weight of the chain was too much.

He struggled wildly, straining at his chains, trying to break free, to get higher up the bank and away from the water; but the iron links held fast.

He was not able to get further away and stared in horror at the silent death gliding lazily towards him. The reptile's hypnotic gaze fixed hungrily on him; dinner wasn't going anywhere.

Max wrenched desperately at his shackles; the chain was heavy, each metal link stronger than he was. He couldn't budge an inch. His legs throbbed where he'd twisted it in his panic and blood ran where metal cut flesh to the bone.

He sobbed and screamed; never had he been so terrified. The alligator was coming out of the water, covered in weed, moving quicker now. Max writhed and bawled and—

He heard a single shot as the reptile leapt forward and flopped on his feet bruising them. Its limbs twitched and the mouth slowly closed on air till it lay like the log it had first resembled.

'A big brute,' Jubilee said.

'Yep!' Dickon spat out a shred of tobacco. 'The kid's earned his dinner. You can feed him.'

But young Max Chaney never heard; he had fainted.

Savage sucked air into his lungs and wished, not for the first time, that his recovery would speed up. He felt stronger, but the exertion left him exhausted. He was still far from fit; coming back from the dead was a wearing business.

Tulip had left for work and he was alone. She'd

warned him the police were joining in the hunt; another reason to ready himself to move out.

The air carried the sounds of movement and voices. He edged open the door to listen; the small cabin could be a trap. The sounds were getting nearer and it was soon obvious that Gruber's men were searching the area.

He slipped outside, closed the door and moved around to the rear of the cabin. He couldn't afford to be trapped in his weakened condition.

Other men were closing in from another direction; it seemed he was at the centre of an encircling movement. He looked up; the cabin had a low roof and he reached up, fingers curling about the overhang. To swing himself up took every ounce of strength he could muster, and he lay flat, gasping for breath.

He heard the hunters approaching and kept still, suppressing ragged breathing.

He listened to Gruber's voice. 'That's the nurse's place – we've already searched there, Lew.'

'Then search it again,' a quiet voice said. It was a voice that carried authority, and Savage wondered about the speaker.

The door of the cabin was flung back with a crash. Boots tramped inside. Gruber shouted, 'He's been here – there's a bandage, and two mugs. She hid Savage here and when I get my hands on that cow she'll wish she'd never been born!'

'But where is he now?' the quiet voice asked.

'Well find him! Spread out, boys – he can't be far away.'

Savage lay motionless, relaxed, breathing through his open mouth and waiting for the hunt to move on. He couldn't stay here: the man called Lew sounded much more dangerous than any of Gruber's bunch.

After a while the sounds of the search faded as the hunters drifted further off. Still Savage didn't move as he silently considered his options.

The best hideaway was out in the open, in full view, but for that he needed a few props and they would take money. A sombrero, he decided; he'd learned a few Spanish phrases on a recent trip south of the border, enough to get by. And he could warn Tulip while equipping himself.


'Goodnight,' she called to the doctor as she left the hospital.

Tulip admired Dr Perry for the work he did; and because he was respected, some of that respect rubbed off on her. She hadn't always been able to walk alone after dark without fear. Bad things could happen to a black woman and the law looked the other way; but that was in the past.

She hurried along, intent on getting home quickly to check on her live-in patient and, in her hurry, took a short cut.

She was humming an old-time banjo tune when an arm reached out from the shadows and pulled her into an alley. A sack came down over her head, muffling her cries. She was jerked roughly along, stumbling, struggling to breathe. Dust got up her nose and she sneezed.

Sounds of the busy street faded and then there was uneven footing and she fell heavily, landing on something that turned her ankle.

She lay helpless, gasping and in pain. A man laughed, and a boot slammed into her side, bringing new pain. The sack was removed and she was hauled upright by her hair; she concentrated on breathing and, after a while, realized there was more than one man involved.

They were shadowy shapes in the dark and her old fears returned. Her heart sank. 'I don't have much in my purse,' she panted. 'Just take it and leave me alone.'

A hand struck her face, drawing blood. Cloud cleared the moon and she recognized the apelike face of Gruber. It wasn't money they were after.

'Bitch,' he grunted. 'Where Savage?'

'I don't know—'

He balled his hand and punched her in the stomach and she doubled over, retching.

'Let me use a knife on her,' another of the gang urged. 'Women don't like having their faces marked. Reckon she'll tell us then.'

Gruber grabbed her hair and pulled her upright again. Now she saw she was on an empty building site; no one was likely to come this way before morning.

He repeated, 'Where's Savage?'

'I don't—'

'Black whore!' He hit her in the face, bringing tears to her eyes. He twisted one arm up behind her back till she cried out.

'Take it easy,' another man said, alarmed. 'She's Perry's nurse and a lot of people—'

'If you're scared, clear off. I don't need help to make a woman talk.' Gruber was in a fury and didn't care who heard him. 'I know what she wants – and she'll tell me before I finish her!'

# CHAPTER 11

## SANCTUARY

Young Max felt miserable. His stomach was not used to a diet consisting mostly of meat. He was being slowly eaten alive by mosquitoes. His legs were sore where the fetters rubbed, and his knee joints throbbed from the violent way he twisted and turned when he tried to avoid snapping jaws.

He was living a nightmare from which there could be no awakening.

Even Jubilee accepted him at Dickon's assessment as 'po' white trash'. Over all hung the smell of decaying meat as the big man skinned alligators for market and tossed what they didn't need into the swamp. The smell got worse day by day and made him heave; he imagined it was like being on a battlefield. He believed he could never forget that smell if he lived to be a hundred.

From time to time he was staked out as bait and learnt again the meaning of fear. The pile of skins grew and Max accepted this was going to be his life until Uncle Dickon missed. Then it would be over.

He had no control at all over his life and discovered that to be powerless was degrading. He was considered less than human by Dickon; bait to be put on a hook. Slowly, hate began to ferment.

Dread of his situation brought vivid dreams. One day he would have power over other men, one day – but when he was awake he knew this was a fantasy with little hope of coming true.

Something stirred the water nearby and he shrank away, giving a little mewing cry and doubling up his legs.

'See that?' Dickon nodded towards him, his voice edged with contempt. 'Scared of a water rat!'

'Them's young bones,' Jubilee said. 'The way he twists and turns, his legs could grow crooked.'

'So?' Dickon spat a brown stream of tobacco juice into the water. 'He can keep still if he chooses. All he does is distract me with his jerking about – and it ain't as if he'll be walking far, is it?'

Savage padded quietly along a backstreet, keeping in shadow. The air was turning chill, the stars hidden by a bank of cloud; stores had oil lamps burning in their windows and the scraping of a fiddle came from a dance hall above a saloon.

Further on he passed a building site and heard sounds of scuffling, and froze. Seconds passed, then through a gap in the cloud, starlight shone on a man struggling to hold a woman down on the ground. Not his business, he decided.

He was about to pass by when the woman lashed out and the man swore.

'You ugly black cow – for that I'll strip the flesh from your bones!'

Savage stopped dead. Gruber's voice. He moved silently, a cat stalking a rat, stealing up on the gang leader; and now he saw who the woman was. Tulip, her nurse's uniform torn, her face bloodied, fighting for her life.

Savage's smile would have frightened a wolf. Gruber could expect no mercy from him. He cast around for a weapon and hefted a half-brick. He came up behind the apeman; his arm rose, then came down with as much force as he could manage. It was enough.

Gruber slumped forward, across the black woman. She wriggled from under him and got to her feet; she was breathing hard but that didn't slow her down. She turned him on his back, moved his legs apart and kicked him hard in the crotch.

'Something to remember me by!'

Savage bent over the unconscious man and helped himself to a wad of banknotes. He unholstered his revolver and passed it to Tulip.

'If anyone attacks you again, use this.'

She nodded, looking around for a target.

'The others seem to have gone. What do we do now? I'd say we're both in trouble.'

'No more than usual,' Savage said. 'Let's find a store that sells clothing, and then a cutler's.'

'When Chaney finds us—'

'Stop worrying, Tulip. No one's going to find us where we're going.'

Chaney didn't feel at home in his hotel room. It wasn't the room itself; he had the best the hotel could boast. But in the nest he'd made above Gruber's gang, he felt safe and whatever he wanted was in its place. Everything was familiar.

Here he felt a temporary visitor, worrying about his bank balance, his only personal contact the redheaded bodyguard. He spread out an architect's plan on the table and invited Boyd to inspect it.

'You're really going then? It seems to me, Mr Chaney, that you're well placed here, and know hardly anybody in San Francisco.'

The blueprint meant little to Boyd; it represented a big house on a hill with a lot of rooms and, as such, didn't impress him.

'It's the design for a mansion,' Chaney said. 'All the swells on Nob Hill have one, so I aim to go one better.'

Boyd merely shrugged; that kind of thinking was

alien to him.

'Mine will be the biggest and best. The foundations have been laid and building started.'

Boyd wondered if his present job was coming to an end but Chaney said, 'I need to be where the rich and powerful are, and they live high on Nob Hill. They're the ones who can help me on my way to Washington – but I'll still need you to watch my back. Perhaps more than ever.'

Boyd wasn't sure he wanted his future mapped out that far ahead. He had an easy job and Chaney paid well, but he'd recently got interested in Alice Hooper and wasn't keen to leave Sacramento.

Chaney's expression changed suddenly, his face clouded by a scowl. 'But first I want Savage dead.'

'Why not forget him? Wherever he is, he can't touch you.'

'I've just found out that Savage is a Pinkerton, hired by my enemies in Washington. I can't have a spy at my back now. He has to die, and the sooner the better, because I've other, more important, things on my mind.'

Savage brought Tulip to Everett's circus by a round-about route in easy stages, making sure nobody saw them. His bandaged head was covered by a sombrero and he carried a heavy bundle well wrapped in oiled cloth.

She had a damaged ankle and limped, her face marked by bruises and a split lip. She wore an outsize calico dress pinned up where it didn't fit.

He had rejected the idea of borrowing a horse; it would have been too easy to track.

The circus train had been shunted on to a spur line outside town, and the big top erected on waste ground close by the coaches and cages. He heard an elephant trumpet and one of the big cats snarl an answer.

A few oil lamps still burned but it was obvious the circus was shutting down for the night. Excited children were being dragged away by their parents, stragglers from the last show crowd. A moon was high and showed a sea of churned-up mud.

Performers were bedding down their animals, roustabouts checking security; a troupe of clowns retreated to their coach. Sounds were muted and the big top loomed against a few twinkling stars.

Savage looked for the gaudiest coach of all, resplendent in vivid reds, blues and gold and a name in ornate letters: EVERETT. He went up two steps, knocked and a voice called out, 'Who is it?'

He opened the door and pushed Tulip in ahead of him, followed her inside and shut the door. The circus boss glanced at them shrewdly.

'I don't know you, do I?'

He was alone, hanging up the coat of his ringmaster's outfit; in a collarless shirt and suspenders, he looked as human as any clerk in a store. He had a head like a polished egg and a waxed moustache.

'We have an act you'll want to book,' Savage said.

'I throw knives, and this lady acts as my human target.'

'Tomorrow,' Everett said. 'Come back in the morning for an audition.

'My assistant is being hunted by thugs and needs a safe place to sleep tonight. A trained nurse could be useful to you.'

Everett studied her face and nodded; he opened the door and shouted, 'Lola!'

Somewhere close a female voice broke off a lullaby and vented a string of curses. While he waited, Savage inspected the coach; part living quarters, part business office, everything was neat and compact and in its place. Comfortable and warm too.

A few minutes later a small woman in overalls burst in. 'This had better be good – I was singing Queenie to sleep.'

Everett waved a hand at Tulip. 'She needs help.'

Lola's face darkened with suspicion as she inspected the nurse's injuries. 'Which bastard did this?' She turned on Savage. 'You?'

'Not me. There's a bunch of toughs after her.'

Lola sniffed. 'Just like men! Gang up on one poor woman. You come with me, dear, and if one of those brutes so much as shows his face, I'll get Queenie to sit on it.'

The two women went out. Savage opened his parcel, took out a knife and stuck it through his belt. He rewrapped the rest and left them with Everett.

Outside, lights were going out and night settled a

dark shroud over the circus. Savage slid into the shadows; he was on his own again and ready to take on the world.

# CHAPTER 12

## TONIO AND TANIA

Max was in continuous pain; his legs had deformed and even limping was difficult. He'd got used to the flies and mosquitoes; he hardly noticed the smell of the swamp any longer and wolfed down whatever food was handed him. But wearing heavy fetters night and day was slowly crippling him. After dark, the pain kept him awake until he was exhausted.

There were times when even Dickon needed a break from routine; then he would produce a bottle of whiskey from the house in the forest and settle to some serious drinking. He never offered Jubilee a drink, just sat holding the bottle and watching Max. Sometimes he would show him the key to the padlock which he kept on a cord around his neck, under his shirt.

'This is it, boy. Bet you think you can creep up

when I'm asleep and grab it.' He laughed slyly, picked up his rifle and squinted at Max through the sights. 'Bet you can't!'

Worse was when he was again chained to the tree trunk by the water's edge as bait for another alligator. Then fear engulfed him. Sometimes he would get cramp and scream – then Dickon would hit him across the face to silence him. Jubilee watched and said nothing.

Even when Max saw those teeth-lined jaws open he couldn't move; the agony in his twisted limbs was too much and tears blurred his vision. Hate bubbled like poison in a witch's brew.

Once, Jubilee climbed to his feet with a knife in his hand and Max thought it was the end. Instead he cut a straight branch from a tree and trimmed it. He gave the stick to Max.

'Lean on this. It'll help.'

Dickon jeered, 'Don't waste your pity on that piece of bait. It's a shame he can't last for ever.'

I'll outlast you, Max told himself. Soon Jubilee would be taking the skins to market, and then there would be only the two of them. He lived for that day.

When Savage returned in the morning, he found the circus folk at breakfast. They were, he thought, a sort of family; performers, roustabouts, the boss, all sat together at one long table under canvas with the cook's kitchen at one end. He collected a mug of coffee and joined them.

Tulip was excited. 'You'll never guess – I bedded down with Queenie, Lola's elephant!'

'Safest place in the circus,' Everett said. His moustache drooped this morning. 'No one fools around with our Queenie.'

'And I'm going to ride her in the ring,' Tulip added. 'Dressed as an Indian princess . . .'

'Any exotic dress is good disguise. Nobody will recognizie her.'

'. . . once Lola's trained Queenie to lift me on to her back!'

'I've signed her on as our nurse,' Everett said.

Savage helped himself to food. 'She's going to be real busy, as part of my act too.'

'All circus people double up at more than one job.' Everett combed his moustache and stood up. 'I'll audition you now if you're ready.'

Outside, Savage set up a wood board and laid out the knives he'd bought from the cutler on a packing case. He positioned Tulip against the board.

'There's no risk if you don't move,' he told her.

'You think you can scare me after what I've seen Doc do with a knife?'

She waited, eyes open and still as a marble angel, but if she turned pale her dark skin didn't show it. He measured off his paces and laid a marker on the ground. A few of the circus folk gathered to watch.

Savage threw the first knife a half inch wide. She didn't flinch so he placed the next closer. One after another the knives flew from his hand, left and right alternating, outlining her figure against the board. He ended with a flourish.

'You've got an eye,' Everett admitted, 'and she's got nerve. We'll dress up the act a bit for the show, and see if the public like it. Do you have a stage name?'

Savage swept off his sombrero, bowed and blew a kiss. '*Sí, señor*, I am Tonio and my assistant is Tania.'

'Sounds familiar.'

'He was the one who showed me how.'

When they were alone, Tulip said, 'Now that's settled, I'll take a look at your head. And where were you last night?'

'You take care of yourself,' Savage said, 'and let me take care of my business – though I'll be taking an extra blanket tonight.'


If it wasn't one thing, it was another. The new governor was finding unexpected problems. Nothing he couldn't cope with, but time-consuming.

He'd been on his way to the *Union* office when Dr Perry intercepted him.

'My nurse, Tulip, is missing. She left the hospital last night and didn't arrive this morning. Nobody's seen her and I've visited her cabin – her bed hasn't been slept in.'

Perry appeared to be genuinely worried, so Chaney practised his smile.

'I shall speak to the chief of police, Doctor. It's too bad that, before my election, certain criminal elements were allowed to run wild. I shall insist on

111

immediate action to make our streets safe for honest citizens. Rely on me, Doctor, a search will be made to locate your nurse, wherever she may be.'

Hiding, he thought as he limped away, bearing down on his stick, followed by his bodyguard. His new life was a juggling act; being governor meant he had to be available. No longer could he use Gruber's gang as a screen.

He didn't need Boyd for this interview. The banker? No, he anticipated a difficulty there, but not the sort to be resolved by gunplay. Lew? Yes, Lew. He stopped abruptly and turned to face the red-haired man.

'Find Lew for me, will you? I don't expect trouble from Hooper and I'll need to meet with him as soon as I've visited Ward's. Say two hours from now, at the hotel.'

Boyd nodded and walked away. If he was disappointed at not seeing Alice Hooper, it didn't show. Chaney watched him go, then continued to the newspaper office.

She was at the front desk, her hair in curls. He supposed she was attractive to some men, and tried out his smile again.

'Alice, I'm here to offer the *Union* an exclusive – my plans as governor. I'm sure your father will be interested, and in return—'

The door of the back room opened and the editor stalked through. 'Aye, and in return?' He jabbed the stem of his pipe at Chaney. 'If you think, just because you're now governor—'

'I'm news, Hooper. Whatever I say or do is news. I know that, and so do you. Listen to me and you'll be the first in print with my personal plans.'

'Aye,' Hooper repeated sourly. 'And in return?'

'In return—' Chaney switched his attention back to Alice. 'I hope this young lady will make it clear to my man Boyd that she has no serious interest in him. That's all.'

'All? Boyd? Your red-haired killer – my daughter!' Hooper had difficulty with the idea that the gunman fancied her. 'If you think, for one moment, I'd allow that cheap shooter to come anywhere near—'

'He's not that cheap,' Chaney observed.

'Dad,' Alice said. 'There's no need to get excited. Mr Boyd has always been polite . . . and I really have no interest in him.'

'Can I rely on that?' Chaney asked.

'Certainly you can. In confidence, I favour Mr Doyle.'

'Doyle!' Hooper looked at his daughter as if he'd never seen her before.

Chaney relaxed. The important thing was to have Boyd move to San Francisco with him. He felt naked without his bodyguard.

'So, now, Mr Hooper, let me inform your readers what they can expect. . . .'

Chaney kept the interview short now he'd got what he wanted, and hired a cab to take him to Ward's.

The small private bank looked like any other brick

house and seemed out of place only because it was tucked away in a back street and didn't advertise. It had a discreet back entrance and a private room that was useful to Chaney and other less-than-scrupulous traders.

As well as lending money at a high rate of interest, Ward financed criminal activities and acquired shares in any new business he calculated stood a chance of success.

A bony man, his gaunt face was adorned by side-burns and he wore a dark business suit with a cravat and pearl stick-pin. He appeared to be in a serious mood.

'Sit down, Chaney, and listen to what I have to say.'

He made no offer of refreshments or enquired about his visitor's health. They both knew this bank dealt exclusively in money in one form or another, and often of an illegal nature.

'I don't see a problem,' Chaney said.

'The problem is that your account is seriously low. Far too much money going out, not nearly enough coming in.'

'I've had extra expenses in the run-up to my election.'

'I don't doubt it.' Ward's tone was dry as sawdust. 'Nevertheless, listen to me. I don't want to be forced to curtail your withdrawals – that would not be good for either of us – but I do need to see something substantial in the way of a deposit.'

Chaney permitted himself a scowl. 'I thought I'd

put enough gold in your bank to last longer than this.'

'Gold has a certain value,' Ward admitted. 'But gold obtained in a less than open manner can attract undesirable attention. It needs to bide its time for exchanging into a more useful currency. Surely you realize that? Only a substantial cash deposit now will solve your problem.'

'And yours apparently.' Chaney turned to leave. 'You can stop worrying, Ward – I'm about to arrange that.'

The banker made a thin smile. 'I'm not the one who should worry. You're the governor, so you can't afford to be seen unable to pay your bills. That wouldn't go down at all well – voters might get the wrong idea.'

'I've a job coming off.'

'Make it soon.' Ward didn't offer to shake hands as he ushered Chaney out.

# CHAPTER 13

## THE KEY

Tulip had forgotten her fear. She was a child again, in a world of wonder. Clowns tumbled, trapeze artistes swung overhead with daring ease, and she was thrilled to be part of it all; a small part, but behind the scenes with the greasepaint and tinsel and a new life opening up before her.

Under the canvas, Lola tapped Queenie with a short stick. 'Kneel.' The elephant's front legs bent as she lowered her great bulk.

'Tulip up,' Lola commanded.

The elephant's trunk curled around Tulip's ample waist and her feet left the ground. She gasped, not really expecting anything to happen; but she soared through the air with no apparent effort and landed on Queenie's back. The trunk uncurled and fell away, leaving her marooned.

'Rise.'

Laboriously Queenie's front legs straightened, and Tulip clutched at bristly hairs.

'Walk.'

Tail swishing, Queenie lurched into forward motion and began to circle the sawdust ring. Tulip clung on. She'd got used to Queenie's smell, so she supposed she would get used to her rolling gait.

Tulip giggled. Lola was tiny, a wisp of a girl, while she was solid with a lot of flesh covering big bones; and Queenie was enormous, a grey mountain lumbering along on thick stumpy legs.

Suddenly she sobered; it seemed a long way to the ground. She concentrated on keeping her balance as her giant mount swayed from side to side. She remembered what Lola had told her and felt better: 'When you sleep with her, Queenie learns your personal scent, and she's protective of people she knows.'

Tulip began to relax and enjoy her ride. Of course, it was only a try-out; the real thing would come later, perhaps.

Lola called quietly to her, using a different tone of voice from the one she used to command her elephant.

'Stand up now. Keep your balance and adjust to the rhythm of her movements.'

Tulip took a deep breath. Now she knew why Lola had insisted she remove her shoes. Carefully, she knelt, then slowly raised herself, her toes trying to curl around Queenie's bristles.

Standing, she circled the ring once more, gaining confidence.

'How's that?' Lola asked the circus boss.

He tweaked his moustache. 'She'll do. Get her dressed for performance.'

As soon as Jubilee loaded the alligator skins into the boat and pushed off, Uncle Dickon brought out a bottle of whiskey and started to drink.

Max watched closely. This was, he realized, a weakness, and any weakness must give him an advantage. He stayed where he was, resting with his back to a tree, gripping the stick Jubilee had cut for him, the stick that lay in the long grass beside him. The stick he hoped Dickon had forgotten. He tried to ignore the chains that weighed him down.

Dickon sprawled at his ease in a wicker chair, grinning. His rifle lay beside him. He opened his shirt and pulled out the key on a cord and dangled it in front of Max's eyes.

'Figured out a way to get this yet? You never will, kid, because I can hold my liquor.'

Max said nothing, wondering why Dickon found it necessary to drink, wondering if his uncle intended to shoot him.

His leg was hurting and he tightened his grip on the stick. Fear would no longer hold him back if he got a chance; fear was now submerged beneath hatred. Wait, he told himself, you'll only get one chance.

They both waited, watching each other, barely stirring in the sticky heat.

Dickon reached the bottom of the bottle and shook it to make sure it was empty. He staggered upright to hurl the empty from him and tottered towards the water's edge.

Taking care not to rattle his chain, Max picked up his stick and leaned forward. He thrust the stick between his uncle's legs. Dickon tripped and stumbled; the edge of the bank crumbled under his weight and he lost his balance and, arms flailing, floundered into the water.

Cursing, he sobered rapidly and struggled to regain the bank. One foot went down an unseen hole and he went under.

Max hauled on his chain, ignoring pain; he was in a hurry now. He dragged himself to the river's edge as Dickon's head came up, his mouth vomiting brown sludge. Max jabbed with his stick, pushing him under.

This time when he came up, struggling to breathe, he choked out, 'Help me, kid. Help me out or, by God, I'll shoot you dead!'

Max extended his stick and, as Dickon groped for it, forced him under again. When he surfaced, Max called, 'Throw me the key and I'll help you. The key first.' Max was smiling; now he was the one with power.

Dickon raved, but one foot seemed embedded in mud, holding him back.

' 'Gator's coming,' Max said, and laughed.

Dickon worked himself into a frenzy. He struggled with the cord around his neck, finally getting it free and tossing it towards the bank.

'Max . . . help me!'

It fell short and Max concentrated on using his stick to fish it out; finally he held the key in his hand.

He'd intended to push his uncle under and hold him there till he drowned, but saw that wasn't necessary. He unlocked the chain and limped away as the first alligator pulled Dickon under. He heard a scream, suddenly cut off, and saw a brief flurry in the water as it turned red.

The boat rocked gently, rocking him to sleep. Despite an extra blanket, Savage was still cold. The small boat he'd borrowed was tied to one of the piers under the old chandler's store Gruber used as headquarters; the one place Savage felt sure his hunters wouldn't look.

It was dark, but not especially so. Light seeped down through cracks in the boards, but no warmth. He catnapped, aware of the smell of garbage, the murmur of water gently lapping at the piers, card calls, swearing and crude jokes. He hadn't heard Chaney's voice.

A door banged, alerting him. A new voice spoke. 'Orders from Mr Chaney—'

Savage rose cautiously, standing to get an ear close to the trapdoor. He could make out the voice, one he'd heard while lying flat on the roof of Tulip's cabin; a quiet voice with a ring of authority. Lew.

Gruber interrupted him. 'Have you found Savage yet, or that black bitch?'

'No sighting of either so far, and the whole force is looking. But they'll surface one day, and then—'

'I want that nurse real bad,' Gruber said, 'and I want her soon. I'm still hurting where she kicked me.'

One of the gang sniggered. 'That's sure one gal you didn't tame!'

'I'll do more than tame her. When I get my hands on her, they'll hear her screaming down in Mexico.'

'Orders!' Lew spoke sharply. 'Mr Chaney wants your outfit to raid the circus. Apparently the tax they pay isn't enough for what he wants – so you're to grab the whole takings. Got that?'

Someone whistled. 'That'll add up to a tidy sum. I guess most of the town has paid good money to see the show.'

'Got it,' Gruber growled.

In the darkness beneath the trapdoor, Savage smiled.


Max went into hiding as soon as he heard the splash of a paddle. He'd chosen the place earlier and had Dickon's rifle with him.

The gun was loaded, the safety off, his hands wet with sweat. Point and pull the trigger he reminded himself; no one had seen him trip Dickon, and there was no one about to see him shoot Jubilee and take the boat.

Jubilee sent his boat gliding to the landing stage and tied up. He called, 'Hi there, Mr Dickon, I'm back.'

Max jerked the trigger and nearly went over backwards. The shot went wild, scaring birds out of their trees.

Jubilee stood still, big in the sunlight. Slowly he took off his straw hat and held it in front of him, as if it might stop bullets.

'Guess that's you, Max. Got free, did you? You ready to try a second shot, or can we talk?' He appeared calm and reasonable.

'I'm free and I've got you covered,' Max said. 'My uncle is dead and I'm taking the boat.'

'There's no call for foolishness, Max. How are you going to find your way out of here unless I guide you? It's not easy to find a route through swampland. You need me, Max.'

Max held his fire.

'Bet you didn't stop to think I might need you as much as you need me. You really think I cut that stick just to help you move about? You've no idea what it's like for a freed slave, have you? There's plenty of Southern whites who don't go along with Northern made laws.'

Max was thinking furiously. 'What d'you mean exactly?'

'I mean we can help each other. I've got provisions

and money in the boat – enough to get me lynched if I'm stopped on my own. I figure you'll head north – take me along with you, anywhere out of the south.'

Max lowered his rifle. What Jubilee said began to make sense. He hadn't really thought about how he'd get away, or where he'd go.

'Take a gamble,' Jubilee urged. 'What have you got to lose if we travel together? North, west, anywhere you say out of here. Guess you're on your own now, right? Is it on?'

Go where? Max thought. He had nowhere to go, nobody to turn to for help. He was alone in the world.

Jubilee said, 'I heard gold was found in California. Maybe we could chance our luck together.'

Gamble? Chance? Luck? Like whiskey, this implied a weakness, a lever to use.

Max nodded. 'Why not? We'll leave together.'

# CHAPTER 14

## NIGHT RAIDERS

The late evening sky was dark with grey clouds hiding the stars. The few oil lamps marking the circus area seemed miles away, and the path Gruber and his men were trying to follow was more like a furrow ploughed in mud. The air was chill and they couldn't move fast enough to keep warm.

Gruber swore as he tripped over a guy rope where there didn't appear to be a need for one. 'Where the hell are we, Smelly?'

'Nearly there, boss. I can just make out the big tent. You said to avoid the crowd.'

Gruber stumbled again. 'I didn't say to lose us in darkest California.'

'A lot of people go to the circus, boss, so a lot of people have to leave. I enjoyed the show, had three seats to myself, 'cause the other people didn't stay long.'

Gruber could understand that. He had a strong desire to light a cheroot, but didn't want to give their position away. The final notes of a brass band died as another of the gang lurched into a pothole and cursed.

Smelly said, 'The money stays in the box office till after the show, then it's taken to the boss's coach.'

Gruber muttered, 'Just lead us to it and keep quiet.'

A family on their way home glanced warily at them stumbling their way towards the circus, and then looked hurriedly away.

Gruber saw the outline of the big top and paused, waiting for his crew to catch up. 'At last. Remember, we don't want trouble – just move in, grab the cash and get out.'

He peered into the gloom. Yellow gleams of lamplight showed here and there as the circus folk retreated to their coaches or animal cages to bed down their charges. It seemed quiet and peaceful as the last of the townspeople disappeared.

'Right. Let's get the money.'

As he started forward, a grey shape loomed in front of him, big as the side of a house and moving. It seemed to be coming straight for him.

'The show must go on!'

This seemed to be the only thing the circus folk

agreed on: they were still arguing in the interval about how to deal with the threat posed by Gruber and his gang, Rivalry was buried; now it was a family matter their ranks closed.

The strong man flexed his muscles and hefted an iron bar; the lion trainer suggested releasing his cats; the clowns proposed to use buckets of water.

Everett said, 'We can't risk our animals, but what we can do is put our takings in a strong box and put that in the cage with the big cats.'

Tulip flourished the revolver Savage had taken from Gruber. 'You needn't think you can keep me away – I owe them one!'

They all seemed determined to meet trouble more than half way. Savage warned, 'These men are killers.'

'Stop worrying, Mr Savage,' Everett said. 'We're grateful for the warning, but this isn't the first time crooks have tried to rob us.'

The show continued to a rousing musical finale and the crowd started to disperse. The animals retired to their cages, restless because they sensed a different atmosphere from usual. Darkness settled over Everett's circus.

Savage, teeth bared in a wolfish smile and knife in hand, waited in shadow. Somewhere, a man tripped over one of the ropes that had been rigged on every likely approach.

A whisper ran around those waiting for action. 'They're coming.'

Vague figures showed in the gloom. The roustabouts waited no longer; they charged, swinging sledge-hammers, and a man screamed as bone splintered.

Red flame stabbed from revolvers. The strong man grabbed two bodies and slammed heads together; the sound drowned out gunshots.

Savage laughed wildly as he lunged with his blade, glad to be active again. He left the knife deep in flesh and used a wrestling hold to discourage another would-be robber, pleased he wasn't out of breath and his head seemed clear. He was gaining confidence rapidly, feeling as good as he'd ever felt. . . .

Gruber froze, petrified, slow to realize that what he saw was a circus elephant.

A bullet missed him by so small a margin the wind of its passing brought him back to reality. He stared at the large woman who'd shot at him; that nurse! He forgot the money, forgot everything except this woman who had humiliated him.

'You! You bloody cow, I'll—'

As he made a grab for her, Queenie trumpeted and lurched forward, ears flapping and trunk swinging. Gruber took a step backwards hurriedly, slipped in the mud and went down.

Queenie reached Tulip and one massive foot came down on Gruber, preventing him from getting up. Her trunk snaked around Tulip's waist, lifting her to safety – and the great bulk of the elephant bore down on Gruber.

His head was pushed deeper into the soft earth. He struggled to breathe and his mouth and nostrils filled with mud. He panicked. As his lungs were deprived of air he made one last effort to heave himself upright before his strength failed.

With Tulip safely on her back, Queenie trumpeted her victory and turned away, heading for her quarters; by then it was too late for Gruber. His gang broke and ran for their lives, any thought of robbery forgotten.

'After them!'

'No! Come back here!'

The circus boss could stop his own men from following, but no one could stop Savage.

Lew, under cover off to one side of the fight, watched the remnants of Gruber's gang scatter as if pursued by wild animals; perhaps they thought they were.

The situation was, from a policeman' point of view, satisfactory, though he didn't believe the new governor would see it that way. He smiled as he thought of Chaney and the way Savage had hidden right under his nose.

Savage was close behind one of the gang who had been hit in the leg; the man staggered along, his breathing ragged. 'Don't leave me – help me!'

But the survivors were only interested in saving their own skins.

Lew moved parallel with Savage, keeping a low profile; and was glad he had when another figure rose up from the ground to confront the fugitive.

'Just take a rest, fella,' drawled a familiar voice. 'I figure someone wants to ask a few questions.'

Doyle. Immediately he recognized the dandy, Lew sank to the ground. Doyle bothered him; he felt sure he wasn't a cowhand or from Texas.

Savage came up, nodded to Doyle and inspected his catch. 'This one isn't going to last long. Are any of the others still about?'

'No one who's likely to stand still long enough to talk. Reckon something scared 'em real bad.'

'That was Queenie.' Savage looked at the injured man. 'So this one'll have to be persuaded.'

Doyle brought a badge from his pocket and showed it. 'US marshal,' he said crisply, 'and I'll do the questioning. There was a fella named Jarvis, who went missing. I want to know what happened to him. If he's dead, I want the name of his killer.'

'I ain't talking,' the injured man said sullenly, 'and you can't make me.'

Savage rammed his boot into the man's injured leg; he screeched and collapsed on the ground, writhing in agony. 'For God's sake, I need a doctor!'

'Wrong,' Savage said. 'You need an undertaker. Just answer the question.'

'That's probably illegal,' Doyle said mildly, 'but I still want to know who killed Don Jarvis.'

The man on the ground got himself under control. 'It was Boyd – Boyd shot him.'

'And who paid Boyd?'

'Who d'you think? Chaney, of course. Now leave me alone.'

Doyle turned to Savage. 'You heard him. You're my witness.'

'For what that's worth. You might convict Boyd, if Chaney disowns him and if you take him alive. But Chaney will laugh at you – he's beyond your reach now he's governor.'

Lew, listening, nodded to himself. Nothing was surer. Max Chaney could wriggle out of anything.

Chaney's leg ached and he lay flat on the bed in his hotel room to rest it. Boyd stood to one side, Lew in front of him. Sometimes he felt the strings weren't working, the puppets not dancing to his tune.

The chief's ferret had finally located Savage, but too late. The damage had been done. There would be no money from the circus to keep Ward quiet.

And Doyle turned out to be a lawman. Did Hooper know that?

Chaney kept a poker face. It might be better to move to San Francisco sooner than later, even if it meant recruiting another gang from scratch. There were plenty of bully-boys there, he'd heard. But he was going to miss Gruber more than he'd let himself acknowledge. The apeman had been useful from their first meeting . . .

. . . Jubilee went from looking happy to wary in one second. He straightened up, flexed his muscles and hefted a pick handle.

'I think we've got trouble, Mr Max.'

The two of them were alone in the hills of California. A stream flowed through a gully and, where sunlight touched the water, flecks of yellow metal sparkled. Maybe it was only something left from another miner's strike, but he didn't think so. Max had a hunch they'd found something worth claiming.

He glanced up and reached for his rifle, checked it was loaded and pushed off the safety. His twisted leg pained him and had put lines in his face; he was no longer a boy.

There were three men, their leader looking like an ape with his long arms: the two flankers held guns. The leader ignored Jubilee.

'How're you going to handle your claim, youngster? We figure you need help and that's what we're offering. We'll protect you and your claim from all-comers and, in return, you need only give us a half-share. What d'yuh say?'

Max watched the man's eyes. There was cunning there, and maybe that was what he needed; cunning to start him on his way to power. Gold, with cunning, could prove a winning combination.

'How many men do you have? How big an area do you cover? What's your name?'

The apeman's eyes blinked. 'You're a cool one – but we don't need the black. Greasers, Chinamen, blacks, we won't tolerate any scum near our gold.'

'You haven't answered my questions.'

'I hire men as I need them, and I move around. Most people call me Gruber.'

Max decided Jubilee had served his purpose and was no longer needed. He inclined his head slightly and Gruber drew a revolver and shot the big Negro in the stomach.

As Jubilee went down, he looked at Max and winced. 'I should have known. You're as bad as your uncle.'

Gruber's men dragged him to the nearest tree, placed a noose about his ankles and threw the other end of the rope over a branch. They hauled him up till his head left the ground and secured the rope.

'We'll leave him as a warning,' Gruber said. 'It saves wasting breath telling people to stay the hell away from here.'

'I believe you,' Max said. 'Now listen to me. I've already filed claim in my name, and it stays that way. I've got plans for the future – you stick with me and you'll do all right . . .'


Chaney sat up on the bed and swung his legs to the floor. He needed Boyd with him, so who could he get to deal with Savage? He wasn't leaving that loose end dangling. Savage had to go. Not Lew, but—

He smiled. 'Lew, you can tell the chief I'll be moving to San Francisco as soon as I'm ready.'

Lew nodded, and left the room. He figured Anderson might be pleased to see the back of this new governor.

*

Boyd watched Alice Hooper come out of the store with a basket on her arm; the sunlight turned her hair to gold and she looked radiant. No woman had stirred his feelings the way Alice did.

He moved along the boardwalk to intercept her, lifted his hat and smiled. 'Can I carry that for you, Miss Alice?'

She stopped, her face serious. 'It's nice of you to offer, Mr Boyd, but there's no need. I can manage, thank you.'

'I may be leaving,' he said. 'Quite soon.' His throat seemed to have dried out, his hearthbeat become erratic. He searched her face for any clue to her feelings, but it remained as blank as a mask.

If she wanted, could he change? What else could he do? He'd always lived by his gun; he knew nothing else and it paid well.

'Then I wish you a good journey—'

A male voice sounded behind him. 'Is this fella bothering you, Alice?'

He swung around, right hand automatically dropping to the butt of his revolver. He almost laughed: surely this dandified Texan wasn't about to challenge him?

'No, Jim, he's not. Mr Boyd has always been polite.'

They glared at each other, like two dogs about to fight over a bone. Suddenly Boyd realized she had an understanding with Doyle, and felt confused. For a moment he stared at his rival; then, abruptly, barked a laugh, turned on a heel and strode away.

# CHAPTER 15

## SHAMBLES AT THE SHAMROCK

The bay at San Francisco was crammed with big ships and small boats half hidden by sea mist; tall masts looked like naked trees sticking up through a belt of off-white cloud.

Harry Fowler was not a happy man at this moment. Not only had he lost his chance at being governor for another four years, but he'd heard that Chaney was moving on to his turf: in fact, on his way. His wife was upset over his alleged gambling debts; if she found out where his money did go . . . well, that didn't bear thinking about. He gave a little shudder.

And this fog made it easy for thieves to make off

with goods, already paid for, being moved from ships to his stores. He'd learnt years before to pay in advance; if he didn't, a rival trader would, or an auction force the price up.

And since he'd opened a small hardware shop for miners, he'd prospered; now he had three stores – one catering for women – and more shelves to fill.

He stood at a window of his office above his biggest store, looking down on a busy street; wreathed in mist, shadow people appeared and disappeared on their unknown errands.

Beside him, Quinn frowned. 'We must take action before Chaney arrives. In Sacramento, he had a gang working for him – we don't want that here.'

'I agree.' Fowler, stout and red-faced, sighed. Nominally he was leader of the vigilance committee, but it was Quinn, young and energetic, who took an active role. One day, the youngster might take over completely – Fowler's thoughts turned more and more to retiring – maybe this was an opportunity to test him. 'What d'you suggest?'

'Make an example of one of the gangs. Round them up and stretch a few necks. Leave 'em dangling for Chaney to see.'

Fowler nodded thoughtfully. 'It would show we mean business. Morris openly boasts of stealing my goods and selling them to rival stores so they can undercut my prices.'

'I know where Morris hangs out – the Shamrock.'

'The Shamrock?' Fowler was alarmed. 'That might

not be such a good idea.'

Quinn said patiently, 'I don't mean we'll raid the place. We walk in quietly, grab Morris and the men with him and take them outside. We'll have a regular court – you can act as judge and pass sentence and hang them straight away.'

Fowler favoured the role of judge, but was still reluctant.

Quinn added, 'There'll be no damage and we'll wear masks. No one will be able to put names to us.'

Fowler thought: but suppose Irish talks to Rose and—?'

'Are you sure you can get Morris without upsetting Irish?'

'I'm sure.'

'Very well, do it tonight. Spread the word.'


'I'm relying on you,' Jim Doyle said. 'As a Federal marshal, my hands are tied, but you're a free agent as long as no one catches you outside the law.'

The deck of the river steamer was filling with passengers about to leave for San Francisco, and Doyle had come to see him off.

'Don was more than another marshal, he was a buddy of mine. Boyd and Chaney killed him, and I want them, so keep in touch.'

'I'll do that,' Savage promised.

'You've seen Hooper's interview in the paper – Chaney's building himself a place on Nob Hill. I've talked to Anderson, and he's pleased – Chaney's absence gives him more scope for his own graft. And I hear that Ward is fuming, so Chaney is likely in some financial trouble.'

'He'll be in real trouble when I catch up with him,' Savage said.

Doyle nodded. 'If Chaney runs true to form, he'll want someone like Gruber to do his rough work. I suggest one place to keep an eye on is the Shamrock.'

The steamer let off a long blast on its whistle and a gruff voice called, 'Last warning. All aboard – we're casting off.'

As Savage walked up the gang plank, Doyle headed for the telegraph office. Ropes were coiled and stowed. The steamer edged out into the current and headed downstream. Most of the crowd disappeared into the saloon below deck.

Savage wasn't much of a drinker and leaned on the rail at the stern, watching Sacramento recede into the past. He contemplated the future; he was fit again, armed with a Bowie in a leather sheath and a shotgun.

He remembered Dr Perry and the pressure Chaney had put on him; he remembered Boyd, the red-haired killer who had almost ended his own life. He thought about Chaney; it was not going to be so easy to get at him now he was governor. Guile was needed.

He stared down at the ship's wash; the rush of water past the paddles was deafening. As he considered ways and means he sniffed the air, and the ripe smell of an unwashed body alerted him. Only one man smelt like that. Gruber's man.

Savage slid sideways, turning, and the blade of a knife clattered against the deck rail.

Smelly grunted in annoyance; he'd anticipated easy meat.

Savage closed with him, gripping the knife hand by the wrist in both hands and smashing it down on the rail.

Smelly howled with pain and the knife slipped from his fingers. Savage kicked it overboard. Smelly, grunting, tried to crush him against the rail, but Savage ducked down to get a grip of his attacker's legs and heaved upwards.

Taken by surprise, Smelly wobbled off-balance. Head first, arms waving uselessly, he went over the side, complaining 'I can't—'

The wash from the ship's paddles filled his mouth and sucked him under. Savage, watching, saw a head bob up and disappear again.

A passenger tapped his shoulder. 'Is that a man overboard?'

'Not accidentally. When I pointed out he needed a bath, he decided he couldn't wait any longer.'

The fog had lifted from the waterfront and the Shamrock blazed with light and reverberated with noise. Its patrons wanted a good time and Irish paid off the city's patrolmen on a weekly basis. Any innocent who wandered in was likely to leave without his wallet or valuables and sometimes a lot of skin.

The vigilantes had turned out in force and Quinn deployed most to cover the back and side exits. He strode in through the front door with half-a-dozen picked men; young, hard and willing to shoot if necessary. They wore masks. In San Francisco, it paid to be wary of official lawmen; no one could predict with certainty which way they'd jump.

The moment he opened the door he smelled opium; there was a haze of smoke and the smell of spilt liquor. A couple of women leaned on a balcony rail at the top of the stairs, and one shouted, 'Raid!'

Quinn lifted a shotgun and spoke clearly. 'We're here for Morris and his gang. Everyone else is free to leave.'

Behind him, determined men levelled rifles and revolvers.

A small woman, neither young nor old, bustled up; she was thin with hair dyed an orange colour and rings on her fingers capable of flaying the skin off a man's face.

'Leave my customers alone,' she ordered. 'I pay plenty for protection and you're not getting any more.'

'We're not here to collect money, Irish. Or make trouble. This is a hanging job.'

The music died away. In one corner of the room a

bunch of men pushed back chairs and reached for their guns.

Irish faced Quinn, hands on hips and a sneer on her face.

'I know your sort – toffs who reckon they're better than the rest of us, but still want my women in your private rooms!'

A single fiddler started to play 'Hangtown Gals' very slowly. Quinn ignored the music as he ignored Irish. He'd spotted Morris and his crowd and waved his vigilantes forward.

Someone unseen began to shoot out the lamps and a number of drinkers rushed for the doors. For a moment, Quinn lost sight of Morris, a bearded giant, and then his feet were swept from under him.

'Man down!'

Vigilantes pressed forward to cover their fallen leader: Morris's men came to meet them, guns spitting lead. One by one, the lamps failed as the unknown carefully shot them out, reducing the amount of light in the Shamock.

'No,' Irish screamed. 'Fight outside if you must, not in here!'

Quinn had lost his gun when someone trampled on his hand. He tried to get up till a boot studded with protruding nails ripped one of his ears.

He curled up, thinking: this wasn't how it was supposed to happen. A knife flashed, followed by a hollow groan. Red flame lanced the shadows and he smelled cordite. A body, wet with blood, fell across him.

He heard the crunch of a club on bone, and winced. A chair smashed and splinters flew. Hardly any lamps were left alight and in the almost-dark men grappled hand-to-hand, clawing, biting, gouging and tearing flesh. Friend or foe didn't seem to matter.

A shotgun blasted, deafening at close-quarters. Quinn crawled towards a door swinging half-open. He heard a concentrated volley of gunfire, squeals of pain, bottles breaking and crawled through a pool of liquid.

Someone gave a high-pitched giggle. There was a loud crack followed by a shower of broken glass from a mirror, and the voice of Irish, bitter, 'You rotten bastards!'

Quinn was starting to wonder if anyone would get out of the Shamrock alive. On the stairs a woman was crying. Now he smelt smoke and saw a small flame dancing; one of the lamps had broken and started a blaze. Fear of fire drove him upright: 'Jeez, got to get out of here,' he mumbled, and forgot about Morris's gang and his vigilantes and lunged for the door. There was a flurry of gunshots and then he was outside in the night air.

It felt good and he cooled down immediately. A hand gripped his shoulder, turning him to the light. He looked into Fowler's face lit by the burning saloon.

'We've got Morris, but Irish isn't going to be pleased.'

By his expression and the tone of voice, Quinn knew immediately he was going to be the one to take the blame.

# CHAPTER 16

## THE LETTER

Max Chaney paced his hotel room, leaning on his stick. It was an airy room with a high ceiling, comfortable furnishings and a view. It was the view that disturbed him.

His introduction to San Francisco had been a letdown; no town band, no red carpet, just one official greeter. The wealthy families on the surrounding hills failed to put in an appearance.

'Just wait,' he told Boyd. 'Once my mansion's complete, they'll flock around me.'

Maybe, his bodyguard thought; crossing the hotel lobby, his sharp ears had caught a mention of 'Chaney's Folly', and a snigger.

Only a few drunks outside a saloon showed any interest in the new governor; if they were hoping for free drinks they were disappointed.

The room was on the second floor, looking down on a civic square. Everything was of the best, except for the view of a scaffold with the body of Morris twisting at the end of a rope. Chaney had no doubt it had been left deliberately where he would see it.

It was notice that the vigilantes would still deal with lawbreakers despite the governor, that they would put their brand of justice ahead of the law.

'Vigilantes are running wild here,' Chaney said. 'and it's an open secret that Fowler's at their head. That gives me a lever.'

He raised his stick in a threatening gesture.

'The law needs to take a stricter line – those Fowler is persecuting must have a fair trial in a court of law. You'll see, once I've dealt with Fowler, the vigilantes will be easy to control.'

'Maybe,' Boyd said. 'But are the rich and powerful on Nob Hill going to allow a bunch of lawbreakers to take over their city?'

'I shall control the gangs. I'll have them working for me, inside the law. But first I have to get the dirt on Fowler and break him.'

Boyd's smile was bleak.

Savage looked at San Francisco with a critical eye as his riverboat entered the bay and headed for a docking area. He saw solid buildings on the surrounding hills, but down below was the usual jumble of wood and iron sheds and ships of all shapes and sizes.

On the jetties, porters pushed barrows loaded with

farm produce and kids tried to grab what they could. An at-home feeling gave him confidence; he'd seen it all before, on a larger scale, in New York.

There was a familiar smell composed of gutted fish and discarded wrappings and crowded humanity. Gulls dive-bombed and swooped upwards with some titbit in their beaks. Savage sniffed the air; there was also the smell of smoke hanging about.

It didn't concern him there had been a fire recently; he knew San Francisco was famous for its fires. He picked up his saddle-bag and shotgun and walked down the gangplank. A hotel? A meal first?

He remembered Doyle's parting words: 'One place to keep an eye on is the Shamrock'. And decided he needed to move fast, before Chaney learnt he was still alive. He asked a dock worker to direct him.

'The Shamrock, is it? What's left of it.' The man lifted a grimy hand and pointed.

Savage followed the pointing arm and then his nose as the smell of smoke grew stronger. Further along the waterfront he saw the burnt-out shell of a saloon and workmen busy with timber, hammers and nails as they began to rebuild.

To one side a small woman with vivid orange hair urged them on with a tongue like a whiplash.

'Stop crawling like a lot of lame turtles! You're here to work, so get the lead out of your boots. You don't fall asleep on the job – I'm paying double the rate because I want the Shamrock to open tonight, not next week!'

Savage touched his hat respectfully. 'What happened, ma'am?'

She glanced sideways at him, saw he was a stranger and put a curb on her tongue. 'Vigilantes happened. Fowler's boys raided us – may he rot in hell! – and I'll make the bastard pay.'

'Fowler? Does Max Chaney know about this?'

'The hell with Chaney, and Fowler, and you, whoever you are! Just get out of my way and let me—'

'I reckon a word in Chaney's ear might get results without you getting involved.'

She paused in her harangue of a workman to look at Savage suspiciously. 'Is that right?' For the first time she gave him serious attention.

'I know Chaney wants to bring Fowler down . . . if someone gives him the ammunition.'

'Well, now, that's interesting.' She drew a long breath. 'Suppose I tell you the real reason Harry Fowler's up to his neck in debt, and it ain't his gambling. Her name is Rose and she spends money – Fowler's money – like he had his own mint. He likely wishes he had, 'cause I'd guess the banks are getting a bit wary of him. Of course, his wife doesn't know. . . .'

Her voice grew resigned. 'It's true, isn't it? The wife is always the last to know!'

Jim Doyle kept to his role as a cowboy from Texas, but there was no point to that at the telegraph office in Sacramento; not when he was expecting a wire from his superior with fresh orders after filing his report.

So when the operator handed him a lengthy message, he was surprised. His boss usually was as mean with words as he was with expenses. He glanced at the name at the end – *Savage* – and raised an eyebrow.

He read the message through, and then read it again. It was not at all what he expected, but he'd known Don Jarvis and was prepared to bend the rules to bring his killers down.

Folding the message form and tucking it in his pocket, he nodded to the operator and left the office. As he walked he considered first one idea, then another, until he hit on a name: Olsen.

Yes, Olsen was the man for this job. He was pleased he'd thought of him, and had no scruples about putting pressure on a crook.

In his role as cowboy he'd spent considerable time playing cards in saloons, and this gave him access to loose tongues. So he knew where to look for the forger.

He made his way to a pawnshop in a back street, where the pawnbroker also acted as a fence for stolen property.

Doyle walked in and showed his badge to One-Eye, a war veteran. 'I'm not after you,' he said, 'so don't bother with any lies. I want to talk to Olsen.'

'I don't know anyone by that name.'

'Of course you don't. The man in your cellar – what name is he using now? This isn't a pinch – I want him to do a job for me.'

'That's different.'

Doyle followed One-Eye along a passage behind the counter. There was a door at the end and steps leading down and the glimmer of an oil lamp at the bottom.

'Mr Olsen, you have a visitor.'

Doyle went down and the door closed behind him. At the bottom was a small room crammed with gear; a grey man sat at a bench, a glass screwed into his eye. Casually he dropped a cloth over what he was working on.

'Mr Doyle, isn't it? I've wondered about you.'

'It's no secret now. Do me a favour and I'll turn a blind eye to whatever you're up to.'

Olsen gave a faint smile. 'Yes? And what is it you want?'

'You're known as a penman. I want you to write a letter, in your best feminine hand. I'll tell you what to write.'

'Do I have a choice?'

Doyle didn't bother to answer as the forger reached for pen and ink and paper. An hour later, he saddled his horse and set off for San Francisco at a fast lope. He was excited, keen to be present when the trap closed on the killers of Don Jarvis.

# CHAPTER 17

## CHANEY'S FOLLY

Savage was sitting in the new Shamrock, making a small beer last. There was a smell of sawdust and whitewash and a cool breeze from windows without glass. Customers stood at a makeshift bar.

When Doyle walked in, Savage called for whiskey and Irish brought a bottle and tumbler and sat down at the table with them. Doyle looked weary, and slumped in his chair; it had been a punishing ride.

Irish filled the tumbler and he tipped back his head and drained it. She refilled it.

'Better,' Doyle said. 'My horse—'

Irish called to one of her helpers. 'Take care of this fella's horse.'

Doyle managed a grin. 'It's nice to be welcome.'

'The letter!'

He handed Olsen's forgery to Savage, who read it and passed it to Irish. 'Looks fine,' he said.

Irish sniffed. 'Why is it men never use their heads?' She took the letter and went behind the bar.

Savage murmured, 'She's got a down on Fowler. Blames him for the fire that gutted this place.'

Doyle nodded, not really interested. He was watching Irish closely.

When she returned, she handed Savage the letter. 'I think you'll find this better.'

His nose wrinkled; she'd spilt a few drops of perfume on it. 'Rose used to work here before she hooked Fowler, and I know she wouldn't send a letter without reminding him of her scent.'

Doyle was impressed. 'So how do we get it to Chaney?' he asked.

'That part's easy. One of my men will deliver it to his hotel.'

Irish's smile was the smile of a cat playing with a mouse as she sealed the letter with a kiss.

Boyd had his feet up, reading a local paper when a knock came at the door. He put his feet down, loosened his revolver in its holster and called, 'Who is it?'

'Hotel deskman. A letter, delivered by hand, for Mr Chaney.'

Boyd opened the door and accepted the letter, closed the door again. He passed it to Chaney, who looked pleased.

'This could be the invitation I want, to meet Nob Hill society.'

He ripped open the letter, read it quickly, and laughed.

'Not this time – it seems somebody doesn't like Harry Fowler.' He passed it to Boyd, who took it with his left hand and read:

*Dearest Harry,*

*I know you don't like me to bother you with money problems, but my allowance goes nowhere. You're always saying I have expensive tastes, but so do you. And you don't really want me heaping up debts in your name, do you?*

*I'm short again, what with the apartment to keep up, the fancy underclothes you like and, of course, your favourite French brandy. I need another $500 quickly.*

*Your everloving Rose.*

Boyd said, 'It could be a trap.'

'You didn't use your nose – it carries a woman's perfume. It's genuine enough.' Chaney seemed eager to believe. 'I've got Fowler where I want him, and he'll take my orders if he doesn't want his wife on his neck.'

Boyd watched a gloating expression develop on his employer's face as he walked up and down.

'This will be better than taking over one of the gangs. I can use Fowler's vigilantes, and nobody will guess their orders come from me. Fowler will take all the responsibility. I'll get a message to him right away to fix a meeting.'

'We choose the meeting place,' Boyd said quickly.

'Of course.' Chaney took up a pen and a sheet of hotel notepaper and started to write.

Boyd watched him with growing doubt. His life had been spent protecting people like Chaney, and he began to see himself as Alice saw him – a gunfighter protecting the wrong people – and he didn't like it.

But he was an honest man in his own way; he'd taken Chaney's money and he would continue to protect him.

Savage, with Doyle, watched from a café window across the street.

'That's my man,' Doyle murmured, nodding towards a dapper figure with a van Dyke beard and a silver-headed cane.

'He doesn't look like an officer.'

'So much the better – Monty can move in the best circles. But criminals know him well enough to be on their guard.'

They'd been waiting and watching since Olsen's letter had been delivered to the hotel. A mist had started to drift inland and soon it would be difficult to see across the road.

The officer moved smoothly as a burly man wearing a derby hat came out of the hotel, whistling. He tapped the man's shoulder with his cane.

'Hello, Pat. You sound cheerful, so what's on? A job, is it?'

'I'm clean, Monty.' Pat spoke with an Australian

accent. 'What I'm on is running an errand for our new governor.'

'Is that so? We'll discuss it at the station – you know the way.'

'Look,' said Pat. 'This is truth – I've got a note to deliver to Mr Fowler.'

Savage and Doyle fell in, one on each side of him. 'That's interesting,' Savage said. 'I think we'd better take a look at it.'

Pat was startled. 'Who the hell are you?'

'Witnesses.'

'To what? I haven't done anything.'

'Witnesses to whatever this officer decides to charge you with,' Doyle said.

'And here's the station, Pat. Inside with you.'

Chaney's messenger was relieved of his gun and the note addressed to Fowler and locked away, still protesting his complete innocence of everything.

Savage broke the seal and read the note aloud:

*Fowler*
*I have a letter from Rose, naming you. Meet me at the*
*site of my mansion, alone, at ten tonight. Ignore this,*
*and the letter will go immediately to your wife.*
*Chaney*

'Nice,' Doyle said. 'Thanks, Monty. If you have a dungeon handy, throw Pat in and forget him for twenty-four hours. Then you can throw him out.'

'Maybe I'll just lose the key.' Monty sounded

disgusted. 'I hate to see scum like that working for our governor!'

Savage said, 'We'll need to visit this site to see the layout. There's no need to bother Mr Fowler – we'll stand in for him tonight.'

When they left the station, the fog was getting thicker.


Chaney's Folly was built high up on a steep hillside. Because of this it had rooms at different levels with stairways between them. The foundations had been completed and some walls were standing, supporting door frames without doors. There were stacks of bricks and tools dropped where workmen had finished for the day.

Savage and Doyle had the place to themselves. At the front was a large hall, empty, with rooms and passages leading off; some rooms had floorboards. The upper rooms were open to the sky and the rear of the building open to the hillside.

The air was cold and Savage skirted patches of mud to avoid leaving tracks. The place was a maze, he thought, ideal: easy to get into, places to hide and spring a surprise.

There was a moon but a fog, drifting up from the sea, made the light tricky. He prowled about with his shotgun, studying the view from different doorways, calculating angles.

Doyle followed him. 'And what is it I'm supposed to do?'

'Keep your head down, look and listen. You'll know when it's your turn – after I deal with Chaney, you can have Boyd.'

'What makes you think this will work?'

'He's expecting Fowler and thinks he's got him under his thumb. That's going to blind him to anything else. Quiet now.'

Doyle sank out of sight behind a half-built wall. Savage waited in the shadow of a pillar supporting overhead timber. It seemed hours since they'd had a meal and he took a bag of raisins from his pocket and began, slowly, to chew a mouthful.

Chaney was impatient, unable to move quicker because of his limp. The evening meal lay heavy in his stomach and the air high up felt cold, taking his breath away.

He walked into the hall of his unfinished mansion, using his stick, and shouted, 'Fowler?' The name echoed several times but there was no other answer. A distant clock chimed the hour of ten. 'Damn the man – he's late.'

Behind him, and a step to one side, Boyd said quietly, 'Lower your voice and stay out of the light.'

'You're jumping at shadows. Fowler doesn't have the guts to try anything.' There was a note of contempt in Chaney's voice.

'Maybe. But someone else might.' Boyd sounded on edge and obviously suspicious.

Fog, thicker now, swirled wraithlike through the

hall, curling around stone columns and creeping over a carpenter's trestle . . .

. . . Savage swallowed as footfalls sounded and Chaney's voice echoed, 'Fowler?'

He moved silently to a new position, keeping Chaney between Boyd and himself. The mist was clammy and brought a chill with it; his fingers were cold on the triggers of his shotgun.

From the bay came the mournful cry of a ship's siren, a sound that vibrated eerily through the Folly. Outside, the branches of trees stirred to make rustling sou nds and send shadows rippling across the floor.

'To hell with Fowler,' Chaney muttered. 'I'll make him pay for keeping me waiting.'

Savage gave a low laugh that sent whispers echoing through the passages and rooms of the Folly without revealing their source.

Boyd spoke tersely. 'It's a trap. Get out of here while I cover you.'

He drew his revolver, searching for a target. The laughter ended and there was only silence. Fog obscured the shadows and the light of the moon faded. He waited, tense.

Before Chaney could move, Savage showed himself, briefly, and called, 'Here!'

Boyd swung around, revolver barrel weaving through an arc, triggering instinctively; but Savage had placed himself so Chaney acted as a shield. Two bullets struck Max Chaney and he cried out, shuddered, and went down, leaking blood.

Savage gave a mocking laugh and Marshal Doyle stepped from cover. 'Drop your gun, Boyd. You're under arrest for the murder of the governor!'

Boyd half-turned, recognizing the man Alice preferred, and bitterness welled up; he determined to force his rival to kill.

'I won't be taken alive,' he shouted wildly.

Savage had placed his shotgun on the ground. In one swift motion he threw his Bowie and Boyd's gun-arm suddenly dangled uselessly at his side, the blade of the knife weighing it down. His revolver hit the floor and exploded harmlessly.

Boyd sighed, swayed in the moonlight, and recovered his poise.

Savage drawled, 'Your prisoner, Jim. I guess you'd prefer to bring him to trial.'

Doyle nodded. 'He got away with killing a marshal, but they'll surely hang him for killing a politician!'